Dedication

To all the single moms struggling to take care of their children. Don't forget that there is always tomorrow.

And as always to my husband, the man who protects and loves me 24/7, 365.

vi

Granny Jo's Journal

Welcome!

WELL, IT'S SPRING on my mountain. The flowers are pushing through the earth, the trees are budding, and the animals and birds are giving birth to the next generation. I must admit that this is my favorite time of year. The air is still fresh and a bit crisp with the remnants of winter, but the sun warms my body and soul enough that I don't need a coat.

I just took a stroll around my yard and was pleased as punch to see green sprouts in my garden and flower beds, a sure sign that the earth is coming back to life after its winter snooze. I'll soon have to start thinking about getting my vegetable garden ready for planting. Oh, and the peace rose on my Earl's grave is starting to bud. That always makes my heart smile.

The only other thing that's new with me is that my granddaughter Becky talked me into buying one of those cell phone thingamajigs. I'm not totally sure how all the fancy stuff on it works, but I have managed to learn how to make a call and say "hello" when it rings. I guess that's good. At my age, you never know when the old body is gonna give out, and you need to cry for help. On the other hand, I'm still not sure I like the idea of people being able to bother me no matter where I am.

Well, enough about me.

I hear tell Davy Collins's wolf, Sadie, just had another litter of puppies. Lydia suspects Sadie made "friends" with the big, male German Shepherd next door. But the animals and birds aren't the only ones expecting additions to their families. My granddaughter Becky is gonna give me another great-grandchild. They tell me this one will be a little girl they plan on naming Josephine. Just thinking about that brings a knot to my throat and a tear to my eye.

I still get such a kick out of doctors being able to tell a mother what her baby is gonna be before it leaves the womb. In my day, you decorated the nursery in yellow or mint green. That way it didn't matter which sex the baby was, and you wouldn't be bedding down a baby boy in a frilly, pink room.

Jonathan and Andi Prince have settled into the big mansion, and I'm still giving Jonathan's Aunt Sarah quilting lessons. Although, she's doing so well, I don't see why she keeps paying me to come there once a week to teach her. I think she just likes the company and someone to gossip with, not that I carry tales, at least not like Laureene Talbot.

Ben Ainsley has retired from the sheriff's office and his son Cole is taking his place until election time rolls around. Cole was a member of the Richmond police force until he came back to Carson a few months ago. So far, from all I've seen (and heard on the grapevine), he's doing a bang-up job, and, if he decides to run in the upcoming election, he'll be a shoo-in for the job on a permanent basis.

Speaking of gossip, Laureene tells me that Faith Chambers, Horace and Celia Chambers' girl, has come home to Carson with her sweet little daughter, Lizzie. Like my Becky, Faith left Carson in search of greener, more exciting pastures. I don't know what exactly brought her back here, but I'm betting that it wasn't anything good. In my experience, young people don't come back here because the opportunities are so great. They're usually hiding from some hurt, and what better place to heal than home? A few months on the mountain should help fix that. There doesn't seem to be any way anyone can live here and not take in the God-given peace of the green hills. It's like an invisible medicine that creeps into your soul and heals its wounds.

As for me, I've got a batch of chocolate chip cookies in the oven right now. Tomorrow, I'll take them over to Faith and Lizzie and see if there's anything I can do for them. Being a single mom nowadays is not an easy row to hoe.

In the meantime, I have a feeling in my bones that things

around here are gonna get interesting. Why? Because it's been quiet for too long and, knowing Carson as I do, I'm waiting for the other shoe to drop. If I was you, I'd stick around . . . just in case my feeling is right.

Love,

—*Granny Jo*

Chapter 1

NOT UNTIL FAITH Chambers stepped off the bus and stood on the main street of Carson, West Virginia, did she fully realize just how dismal her life had become. Three years ago, she'd run from her domineering mother, left her hometown with a head full of dreams and plans, and moved to Atlanta. Once there, she'd taken up with city boy Sloan Philips and settled in, determined never to step foot in this sleepy little town again, and looking forward to a bright tomorrow. Today, alone, nearly penniless, with nothing but gloom on the horizon and two-year-old Lizzie to care for, Faith had returned to her hometown with her tail between her legs, prepared to beg for a job to support them.

"Faith Chambers, is that you?"

Faith turned toward the strident female voice and looked into the judgmental face of her mother's next door neighbor and the town gossip, Laureene Talbot. Lord, of all the people Faith had to run into, why did it have to be her? She'd hoped to slip into town unnoticed. Now, not only was she found out, but this woman would make certain that Faith's mother knew her daughter was back.

"Yes, ma'am, it's me." Faith hugged her two-year-old daughter closer to her chest and forced a smile.

"Well, bless my soul, I certainly never expected to see you back in Carson. And who's this sweet little thing?" She took a step closer and pinched Lizzie's cheek. The child pulled away, hugged her teddy bear closer, and buried her face in Faith's neck. Fuzzy the teddy bear was unique. He'd been made just for Faith by her beloved gramma, and she'd passed it down to Lizzie, who cherished it even more than Faith had and hid behind it whenever anything disturbed her.

Faith figured she'd have to face this woman sooner or later, but she'd hoped it would be later. If Carson was the same as she remembered it, even though a new century had dawned, its moral standards about certain things remained unforgiving by some—Laureene being one of them.

No sense in trying to hide it. Everyone would know soon enough. Taking a deep breath, Faith raised her chin and looked the woman in the eye. "She's my daughter."

Laureene stared at the child for a moment, as if deep in thought. "I don't recall your momma telling me that you got married or that you gave her a grandbaby. Who's the lucky daddy?" The woman's a sweet expression covered the vindictive personality that Faith was well aware lurked just beneath the surface.

Faith wasn't surprised that her mother hadn't told anyone about Lizzie or that Faith had been living "in sin" with a city man. Celia Chambers had known about Sloan and Lizzie, but Faith had no doubt that her mother would not have shared that news with anyone in Carson. Small towns could be cruel about things like illegitimate children and unmarried liaisons. Carson's high moral values made it especially so, even in this century of permissiveness. All that aside, Faith knew her mother would never brag about something she felt was a sin before God and certainly not to Poison Tongue Laureene, as the kids always called her.

Pure and simple, Laureene Talbot was the cruelest kind of small-town gossip. She spread what she knew for sure and made up what she thought was the true story, right or wrong. The results usually ended up being more hurtful than the truth would have been.

When Faith was younger, she would have tried to satisfy Laureene's nosiness with some half-baked excuse, and hope that the story wasn't embellished when Laureene passed it along. But right now, exhausted from the long bus ride from Atlanta, and apprehensive about her and Lizzie's future, Faith didn't have the emotional strength to contend with Laureene Talbot. But neither would she supply grist for Laureene's gossip mill.

Faith straightened her shoulders and smiled as sweetly as she could. "Maybe it slipped her mind."

Laureene's eyebrows shot up so far they nearly touched the wave of black hair draped neatly over her forehead. "That doesn't seem likely. Grandmothers don't forget their grandchildren."

"No, most don't." But her mother was far from being like most grandmothers. Without further explanation, Faith picked up her only suitcase and stepped around Laureene, leaving her, mouth agape, in the middle of the sidewalk.

Once she'd moved out of reach of Laureene's sharp tongue and condemning eyes, Faith breathed a deep sigh of relief. There had been a time when she would have given Laureene as good as she dealt out, but Faith hadn't stood up for herself in so long, she wasn't sure she knew how anymore.

But one thing she did know, she would never again depend on anyone else to take care of her and Lizzie. The day the police knocked on her door and told her Sloan had been killed, probably by one of his drug connections, Faith had realized she was on her own. It was also then that she finally admitted to herself that she and Lizzie had been abandoned emotionally for a long time.

Crossing the street, she hoisted Lizzie higher on her hip and headed for the building with the white sign hanging out front that read Doctor Amos Joseph, MD. Until the new clinic had been built in Hanover a few years back, he'd been the only doctor in the isolated valley, and still, the clinic was over fifty miles away. As a result, Doc Amos had been an indispensable necessity in Carson for many years now. He had delivered Faith and most of the other kids in town, as well as treated most of the town's population at one time or another.

Faith remembered him as being a kind, friendly man with a cheery smile and a never-ending supply of red lollipops hidden away in his big roll-top desk. He'd dispensed wisdom and kindness as readily as he did his candy, medicines, and rainbow-colored bandages. Everyone in town knew that Doc was just as quick to accept a plump roasting chicken as payment for an office visit from a family that was down on their luck as he was to take hard cash.

When she'd noted his name on the classified ad she'd found in the local paper she'd picked from the trash in the bus terminal, it had made her feel better about applying for the job of housekeeper, the only marketable skill she possessed.

Taking a deep breath, she climbed the stairs and entered his office.

It smelled of antiseptic, the flower-scented room deodorizer protruding from an outlet near the door, and stale pipe tobacco. Faith recognized the woman behind the desk as Harriet, Doc's wife and receptionist of over forty years, though her hair was whiter and her cherub-like face more wrinkled,.

Setting her suitcase down beside the door and then shifting Lizzie to a more comfortable position on her hip, Faith approached the desk. Lizzie held her tattered old teddy bear Fuzzy against her cheek, surveyed her new surroundings with wide eyes, and held on tight to the collar of Faith's blouse.

Doc's wife looked up. "Yes? May I help you?"

"I've come to see about the job in the newspaper." Faith held out the dog-eared edition of *The Carson Gazette* she'd pulled from her shoulder bag. "I'm Faith Chambers."

Harriet's eyes widened. "Well, bless me, yes you are. Now, why didn't I recognize you right off?" She rose and came around the desk to gently hug both Lizzie and Faith. "Doc keeps telling me to have my glasses changed, I guess he's right." She grinned, then cupped her hand over her mouth and whispered, "Don't tell him that. He loves it when he's right, and then there's no living with him at all."

Harriet's warm greeting took away the sting of Laureene Talbot's prying. Faith returned the smile and promised, "I won't tell him."

"Good." Not one to waste too much time on social pleasantries, Harriet got right to the heart of the matter. "About that job, dear . . . I'm afraid we hired someone a few days ago. I'm getting too old to run the office and keep up with the chores at home." She leaned closer to Faith. "Truth be told, I'd rather be here anyway. Always hated housework."

The job was filled?

Faith felt the bottom drop out of her world. What would she do now? "Would you or Doc know of anyone looking to hire in Carson? I don't have a car, so I'd need one within walking distance."

"I don't recall any off hand, but Doc might know of something." She lowered her voice as if to share a confidence. "Everybody who comes in here thinks they have to tell him the story of their lives. Between you and me, I think he enjoys hearing the latest about all of them." She grinned. "If anyone in Carson is looking for help, he'll know." She reached across the desk for Doc's brown leather appointment book. "You came at a good time. He doesn't have another appointment for fifteen minutes or so. Get right in there."

Faith looked around the waiting room. "Can I leave Lizzie out here with you? She's sleepy so she shouldn't be any trouble. If it's okay, I'll just lay her on the couch."

Harriet frowned. "You most certainly will not." Faith's heart sank. How was she going to talk to Doc about a job with Lizzie demanding her attention? "She can sit right here on my lap," Harriet said, reaching for Lizzie. "I can never hold the little ones enough."

Lizzie went to Harriet without a backward look at her mother.

"Thank you."

Harriet dismissed Faith's gratitude with a wave of her hand. "No need to thank me. I'll enjoy this more than she will. Now, you get in there and pick Amos's brain about that job."

Heart in her throat, Faith opened the door to Doc's inner office. Just the thought of having to crawl back to her parents and beg them to take her in made her stomach sour. If she didn't get a job, facing her mother's censure and I-told-you-so's would be infinitely worse than facing the entire town's disapproval. She'd rather die than have to crawl home to Celia Chambers.

ACTING SHERIFF Cole Ainsley closed the door to his office,

leaving his deputy, Graylin Talbot, to oversee things in his absence. Even since Davy Collins went missing a while back, before Cole arrived in town, things around Carson had been quiet, with only a few speeding tickets and Jimmy Logan's nightly incarceration for public intoxication to contend with.

A good thing it was, since Graylin would not have been Cole's first choice for Deputy of the Year. His nickname around town was Barney Fife, which kind of said it all. Not that Graylin wasn't a good man and a fine officer, he was. He was just overeager sometimes and lacking a bit in the common sense department. Like the time he arrested Lucas Michaels and Amantha James for "killing" a mechanical baby. Secretly, Cole believed Graylin watched too many cop shows on TV and was just waiting for a serial killer to show up or a crime spree to erupt in Carson—the very last thing Cole wanted. He'd had enough of that kind of life as a detective in Richmond, VA.

Cole glanced across Main Street at the blue SUV that had just maneuvered into the parking slot in front of Keeler's Market. He recognized the car as that of Hunter and Rose Mackenzie. Rose was ready to deliver their third child in a few months, and Hunter had been sticking to her like glue on a postage stamp for the past week to make sure his wife and baby were safe and secure.

Cole felt a pang of jealousy arrow through him. What he wouldn't give to be in Hunter's shoes with a quiet existence, a beautiful wife, two toddlers at home, and a child on the way. Cole had come close to getting some of that, but . . .

If only Diane hadn't waited until he'd fallen in love with her to tell him she had no desire to be married or have children and that her career would always come before a relationship and family. The pain she'd inflicted had gouged a wound deep in his soul. One that still lay raw in his gut. Added to that was the emotional strain the big city crimes he'd witnessed had put on him. He'd seen enough waste of humanity to last him a lifetime.

When his father's health had forced him to leave the sheriff's office before his term was over, and he'd called on Cole to fill in for him until the November elections, Cole had jumped at it. He'd hoped that coming back to Carson would help heal his emotional wounds and give him the quiet life he longed for. Unfortunately, the small, close-knit community, although quiet, held too many reminders of the life Diane had stolen from him. As a result, he'd decided to get out of law enforcement and put his teaching degree to work. After the town's election took place and they had a new sheriff, he planned to take the job he'd been offered teaching history at a high school in Atlanta. Maybe then he could find the peace he sought. Until that time . . .

Shaking his head to free himself of his troubling thoughts, he waved at the Mackenzies, and then hurried down the street toward Doc Amos's office. This should be the last time he'd have to see Doc. The cut on his leg, where he'd had a fight with some barbed wire and lost, had taken weeks to heal, but with Doc's care, it was no more than a thick, pink line running down his calf. Doc being Doc, he wanted one more look before he declared Cole officially healed. Cole had no choice but to reluctantly oblige the good doctor.

Pushing open the office door, Cole found Harriet with a small child balanced on her knee who had a stranglehold on a teddy bear that was nearly as big as she was. The child had crimson saliva dribbling down her chin and over her fingers from the cherry lollipop she waved precariously close to Harriet's hair. Traces of lollipop juice matted the fur on the teddy bear in her free hand.

"Who's your friend, Harriet?" Cole asked.

Harriet never removed her gaze from the child. She tucked her under the chin, and the little girl giggled around the lollipop, which was now jutting from her mouth. "This is Lizzie."

"Lizzie, huh?" The sound of her name brought the little girl's chocolate-brown gaze to him. Her lips were deep red from the candy, and the gold ringlets sticking to her pink cheeks attested to a few encounters with the sticky sweet. He smiled at her, and her angel face broke into a huge grin.

She held the lollipop out to him. "Bites." Cole shook his head and patted his stomach. "No thanks, sweetie. I'm watching my figure." She stared at him for a moment, and then her mouth screwed up into what promised to be a wail of disapproval if he didn't cooperate. "Okay, since you put it that way." Leaning over, he pretended to lick the pop. "Mmm. That's sooo good." Exaggerating the gesture, he smacked his lips loudly. "Thank you."

Lizzie giggled, and then went back to enjoying her lollipop, but kept a sharp eye on Cole.

He traced his finger over her soft, sticky cheek. "Who does this little beauty belong to?"

"She's mine."

Cole straightened and glanced in the direction of the melodic voice. His breath lodged somewhere between his lungs and his throat. Not until the pain pushed at his chest did it dawn on him that he'd have to breathe to find relief.

A little too thin and looking like a fragile piece of porcelain that would shatter under the slightest pressure, the woman scooping Lizzie off Harriet's lap was the most beautiful thing Cole had ever seen, despite the distinct look of defeat in her eyes. With hair the color of summer wheat and eyes that would rival any clear blue sky, she quite literally took his breath away. Without conscious thought, his gaze went to her bare ring finger.

"Cole, this is Faith Chambers." Doc Amos laid a hand on Faith's shoulder, as if protecting her from some unseen danger.

Cole, who hadn't even noticed the good doctor until he spoke, searched for his voice. While he waited for it to come back, he realized how scared she looked. He decided instantly that if she needed protecting from whatever, he wanted to be the one to do it.

He dipped his head. "Ms. Chambers." "Faith, this is Sheriff Ainsley, Ben's son. Faith here's come back to Carson, and she's looking for a job. Don't happen to know of any, do you, Cole?"

He thought for a moment, and then shook his head. "Not off hand."

Despite sounding alert to the conversation, Cole's brain kept replaying something Doc had said. *Back to Carson.*

She'd lived here before?

He searched his memory for any hint that he knew this woman, but nothing registered. Then he recalled a rather pretty, but shy and slender girl a few years behind him in school. He'd often caught those beautiful blue eyes staring at him in the cafeteria or at a sporting event. But that was about it. After all, he'd been eighteen back then, and she'd been . . . What? Maybe fifteen. *Jail bait,* as his friend Jimmy Williams would have said.

One thing for sure, she might have been classified as cute back then, but she'd matured into absolutely stunning. Cole sucked in another steadying breath.

Doc released his grip on Faith's shoulder and drew his pipe from the pocket of his white smock. He cast a glance at Harriet, who frowned, and he immediately returned the pipe to his pocket. "I was just going to ask Harriet to drive Faith out to our cottage north of town. She's gonna stay there until she can find a job and her own place. Now that Harriet's sister is in the nursing home, it just stands there empty. I'd rather have somebody living in it."

"No need to bother Harriet," Cole quickly put in. "I'm heading in that direction anyway. I'd be happy to take Faith and Lizzie out there." He really wasn't going anywhere near there, but he couldn't pass up a chance to spend a little more time with this woman.

Faith opened her mouth to say something, but Doc cut her short. "I kind of figured you might." Doc grinned, obviously on to him, and turned to Faith. "That's probably best. Harriet doesn't know a breaker box from a cereal box. Cole can turn everything on for you. The place is furnished—bed linens, towels, dishes and all. There might even be a crib in the attic for the little one. Harriet never throws anything away." He rolled his eyes in the direction of his wife. "Cole can take you by Keeler's Market for food on the way. Tell Bill I said to put it on my tab, and you can pay me when you get your first week's paycheck."

Faith thanked Doc and Harriet for their generous help, and then glanced at Cole, as if to get his okay. He nodded.

"Since it's right on the way, maybe Faith would like to stop by and see her folks." Harriet stood up and came around the desk to stand beside Doc, who threw his arm around her shoulders.

"Oh, no!" Faith swallowed, and then smiled nervously. The last thing she wanted was to start her new life with a visit with her sanctimonious mother. "I'm . . . I'm tired and so is Lizzie. I think we'd like to settle in. I can see my folks another time. Maybe tomorrow."

Strange. She'd just come back to town and didn't seem in any particular hurry to see her family. When Cole had come back to Carson, he could barely wait to get off the bus and sit down to one of his momma's home-cooked meals.

Glancing at Doc, Cole raised an inquiring eyebrow. Doc shook his head very subtly, as if to say, "Don't push the issue."

"Sounds like a plan to me. Is this yours?" Cole pointed at the battered, brown suitcase sitting beside the door.

Faith nodded.

Grabbing the suitcase, Cole opened the door and stepped to the side for Faith to walk ahead of him. She paused and turned back to Doc and Harriet. "I don't know how to thank you . . . for everything."

"No need," Doc said, easily dismissing her gratitude with a wave of his hand. He frowned at Cole. "Just a minute, Sheriff. Aren't you forgetting your appointment with me?"

Cole was stunned that, in the course of a few minutes, this woman had made him forget. He rarely forgot anything, but she seemed to have changed that, for now anyway. "I'll reschedule."

"No need," Doc declared.

He strode over to where Cole stood. Without preamble, Doc yanked up the leg of Cole's khaki uniform pants. He ran the tip of his finger down the pink line of skin that extended from Cole's mid-calf almost to his ankle. The doctor prodded the scar a few times and then felt the skin around it.

Straightening, he smiled at Cole. "You're gonna have one nasty scar, but I think you'll live. No need for any more visits, unless you decide to out wrestle another piece of barbed wire."

"Not in this lifetime. Once was enough for me." Cole turned to Faith. "Guess that means we can go."

Without a word, Faith strode past Cole. Lizzie grinned up at him, while clinging to her bear with one hand and mother's blouse with the other and leaving tiny red fingerprints on the white material.

He set the suitcase down on the sidewalk, and then turned to Faith. "You wait here. I just have to run down to the office and get the car. Won't take but a minute." She nodded, and then he took off at a trot toward the other side of the street.

Faith watched him as she sorted through the emotions running rampant through her mind and body. She'd needed no reminders of the muscular quarterback on the high school football team that had captured her attention and her heart back then . . . a lifetime ago. And here he was again, all grown up and more handsome than ever.

She took a deep steadying breath. Had coming back to Carson really been such a good idea after all?

Chapter 2

WHILE FAITH WAITED for Cole to return, she thought about the man and the scar on his leg. He'd made light of it, but judging by how angry the scar looked, the injury that caused it must have been very painful. Too bad such a good-looking man had to be disfigured. But then, she found that she liked the idea that Cole wasn't perfect. It made him more human, more approachable, more . . . *No!* She couldn't go there. Everyone had scars, some more than others, and some that couldn't be seen.

The handsome sheriff and Doc Amos had shown her more kindness than she'd seen in the last few years. But it was only kindness. Nothing more. Carson had always looked after its own. She'd do well to remember that. And right now, her battered emotions could use all of the TLC anyone doled out to her.

While she waited for the sheriff to come back, she sorted through long-forgotten memories.

Cole might not remember her, but she certainly remembered him. Images of him surrounded by adoring teenage school girls after a Friday night football game drifted through her mind. He'd exuded charm back then, and, even if he hadn't noticed her, she'd soaked it up like a dry sponge.

But Sloan Phillips had oozed charm, too, when she'd first met him in the small sandwich shop outside the Greyhound Terminal on the day she'd arrived in Atlanta. Wide-eyed, a bit scared, and totally in awe of the big city, she'd been flattered that this handsome stranger had offered to take her under his wing and introduce her to her new hometown. She'd moved into his apartment, temporarily, and never moved out until yesterday when she and Lizzie had left Atlanta.

Faith had fallen hard for Sloan's good looks and charm.

And look where that had gotten her . . . a single, penniless mother reduced to living off the charity of others.

No, it was better for everyone if she kept the sheriff at arm's length. She'd been bitten once by male charisma. Now she knew that a handsome face and a breathtaking smile didn't always mean the man behind it was happiness material.

She pushed Cole from her mind and concentrated on the life she'd make for her and her daughter in Carson. Maybe she and Lizzie could finally find a little happiness to call their own. Faith wasn't thrilled about taking charity from Doc, and only after he'd promised to let her pay rent as soon as she found work, had she agreed to move into the cottage. She smiled, knowing she had at least two friends in Carson.

Then she raised her gaze to follow the sheriff's retreating figure and amended that number to a possible three. Cole sure was a handsome man, what with his nut-brown skin, whiskey eyes, and coal black hair. The kind of man women flocked around. But, she reminded herself, not this woman. Friendship it would be. Nothing more.

Faith had had her fill of handsome men. Sloan had swept her up in his dreams of making a fortune, dreams that included her, dreams of a golden tomorrow. Always making plans for the "big deal" that never materialized. Finally free of her stifling mother and her strict rules and religious do's and don'ts, Faith had foolishly believed in his promises and prepared to begin a glorious, happy future.

Little had she known the night that naïve country girl climbed into Sloan's car with her battered suitcase and impossible fantasies where it would lead. It never crossed her mind that they would be driving toward a future filled with heartache for both of them and a tomorrow that never came.

But Sloan was permanently out of their lives now, and she had to stop thinking about him.

No matter how handsome and charming Cole was, she could not, would not allow herself to fall into that trap again.

The sharp pain of Lizzie trying to untangle her sticky fingers from her mother's hair yanked Faith from her dismal past. Just then, the black and white sheriff's car pulled up at the curb beside her and the object of her musings jumped out and smiled at her. Deep down inside, a spot that had grown cold and numb warmed just a fraction.

Faith pulled her gaze away. She didn't want to feel anything for Cole. Didn't want to acknowledge that he might have the power to stir up her emotions.

Cole moved to the back of the car, opened the trunk, and then pulled out a child's car seat.

"For the smaller prisoners?" she asked with a smile.

He returned her smile with a broad grin that made her heart beat faster. "My sister Karen has me fetch my nephew from daycare a couple of times a week, and it's easier if I have my own baby paraphernalia. So, I keep a car seat in the patrol car."

Still smiling at the idea of a baby seat perched in the back seat of a patrol car, Faith nodded and watched him secure the seat in place. Then he turned to her and lifted Lizzie from her arms. Gently, he strapped her and the bear in, and then ruffled her hair. Lizzie looked up at him with adoring eyes and flashed her toothy grin.

"She likes you," Faith observed.

That surprised her. Normally Lizzie shied away from men, especially big men. The sheriff seemed to be quickly becoming one of her daughter's favorite people in a very short time. It didn't look like Lizzie would have a problem settling into Carson. Faith had a funny feeling it wasn't going to be quite that easy for her.

"That's good. I think I can get pretty fond of her, too."

Before Faith could say anything, a female voice interrupted her. "Lord, I don't know where my mind is these days." They both turned to find Harriet rushing down the front walk toward them carrying a facecloth. "Just hang on a minute. We need to wipe that baby's hands off."

Faith stepped forward to take the cloth, but Cole beat her to it. He bent back into the car, and gently cleaned Lizzie's sticky fingers. As he worked, Lizzie gazed up at him with worshipful, bright eyes. Faith couldn't help but notice how good he was with her small daughter. Sloan had barely acknowledged his daughter's existence. He'd been too busy looking for ways to get rich.

When Cole tickled the child under the chin, then kissed her forehead, Lizzie giggled out loud. Well, Cole had certainly charmed one female in this family. And one was more than enough, Faith decided, then abruptly got into the car.

Cole returned the cloth to Harriet, who waved at them both before turning back to Doc's office. After slipping behind the wheel, Cole inserted the key in the ignition. The powerful engine roared to life, and the car eased away from the curb. Faith plastered herself against the passenger's door, as far as the confining space would allow her, to distance herself from the big magnetic man behind the wheel.

KEELER'S MARKET was crowded with shoppers picking up last-minute items before going home for supper. Cole had placed Lizzie in the baby seat of the shopping cart and pushed it toward the end aisle. The front wheel chattered like a nervous cat in a room full of pit bulls. That he took this chore for granted ruffled Faith's feathers. She wasn't used to a man helping her shop. Sloan had never even gone in a grocery store with her.

"Woman's work," he'd say, and then he'd sit in the car while she and Lizzie did the shopping. He hadn't even gotten out long enough to help her transfer the bags to the trunk of the car. His big contribution had been to push the button on the dashboard to open the trunk.

Faith, who had sworn she wouldn't let anyone take over her life again, roused from her memories and placed a hand on the handle of the cart. "I can do that."

Without interrupting his forward movement, he grinned down at her. "No need. You're probably tired and want to get this done so you can settle in at the house. If I push this cantankerous thing and you put the groceries in it, we can be finished in a flash."

He continued down the aisle. Unable to summon a

reasonable argument for his logic, Faith watched him maneuver the cart in and out of shoppers, leaving her no choice but to follow helplessly behind. By the time she'd caught up to him, he already had milk and bread in the cart, along with a bag of red lollipops.

"How do you know I want this stuff?" she asked crisply.

Again, he flashed his heart-stopping grin at her. "Being a bachelor, I *have* shopped for myself a few times. Besides, since the cupboards are bare in Doc's cottage, it's a safe assumption that you'll need bread and milk." He smoothed Lizzie's pink cheek with his thumb. "And then there are the staples, like cherry lollipops for this beautiful young lady with the sweet tooth." Lizzie giggled and kicked her feet.

Traitor, Faith thought. How was she going to keep this man at a distance if her own daughter wouldn't cooperate? And how could she possibly argue with his logic?

"Well, I'd appreciate it if you'd let me do my own shopping." Faith hated that her voice sounded so harsh, but something told her that Cole didn't understand subtlety.

He considered her for a moment, and then, as if he understood that this small concession was important to her, he nodded. "You got it."

The rest of the shopping trip went smoothly. Cole pushed the cart, and Faith chose the items that went into it, making sure they were inexpensive essentials so that the bill wouldn't be too high. Occasionally, he'd slip something into the grocery cart. When she would frown at him, he'd say he was picking up some things he needed as well. It would save him a trip later. She believed him until they got to the checkout, and he heaped everything together on the conveyer belt.

"You need to keep your stuff separate," she told him. "Remember, this is going on Doc's tab until I get paid."

"Well, I've been thinking about that, and that's gonna make a lot of extra bookkeeping for Harriet. So, if I pay for everything, then you can pay me."

The last thing she wanted was to make any work for Harriet. She and Doc had been so good about extending her this credit so she and Lizzie would have food in the house until she found a job. But she also didn't want to be beholden to Cole. Besides, his solution didn't sound all that simple to her. On the other hand, she wasn't about to make a scene in the middle of the store, and if she and Lizzie were to eat, she'd have to give in on this one point.

"All right, but make sure you keep the register receipt. When we get in the car, I'll mark off what's mine so you know what I owe you."

He nodded and continued to pile the groceries on the belt. When he finished, he hoisted Lizzie from the cart and held her to him. To Faith's astonishment, Lizzie nuzzled her face into his neck and closed her eyes. In seconds, she was asleep.

With amazing agility, he juggled the sleeping child, fished out his wallet, and paid the cashier, then shoved the receipt in his pocket, never disturbing the child on his shoulder. Faith stationed herself at the front of the loaded cart and, when the last bag of groceries was placed in it, she started pushing it toward the automatic exit doors.

"I can get that," Cole declared.

She looked at him with the kind of expression she reserved for Lizzie's more rebellious moments. "And do you take over holding the world on your shoulders for Atlas on weekends?"

Faith planted her feet firmly in front of the grocery cart. "Let's get this straight up front. I can take care of Lizzie and myself. I don't need anyone's help." *Least of all from a man,* she added silently. For a moment, he stared blankly at her, then what she'd said must have registered, and he laughed. "Okay. Point taken."

With Faith in the lead pushing the cart and Cole carrying Lizzie, they headed for the exit as if they were any other little family doing their weekly grocery shopping. The perfect picture had one serious flaw—they weren't a happy little family and never would be. Should she remind Cole of that? She decided to let it pass. Contrarily, having been the sole caregiver to Sloan and Lizzie for so long, she found she liked being the one receiving the care for a change. But she'd never tell him that, and if she wanted to make it on her own, she had to stand her ground against this controlling man and assert her independence.

They'd nearly made it to Cole's car when a black, beat-up sedan pulled up at a crazy angle into a parking spot near them. A man emerged. His beard-shadowed face was flushed, and his clothes showed signs of having been slept in. He staggered a bit before catching his balance.

Bleary-eyed, he studied Faith. "Well, ain't you just the purtiest little thing that's hit these parts in a dog's age." He swayed and clutched at the fender of his car. "How'd you get yourself such a cute little thing, Sheriff?"

Faith drew back. The sight of this man brought back vivid memories of Sloan coming home after a night of partying with his new friends. How his fetid breath reeked of booze, and his drunken snoring would keep her awake for hours.

The man lurched toward her, his hand outstretched. She recognized him as Jimmy Logan, the town drunk. Some things never changed. "Com'ere, sweet thing, and let me get a better look at ya."

Before she could even react, Cole placed himself between them. Carefully, he shifted Lizzie into Faith's arms, and then turned back to the man. "Jimmy, unless you want to lose a hand, you'd better not touch the young lady or the child. Now, give me your keys." Cole held out his hand, palm up. Jimmy stared at Cole's outstretched hand, and then shook his head. "Your keys, Jimmy." The wobbly man shook his head again. "Jimmy, pretty soon I'm gonna stop asking nice, so you best give me the keys before I lose my sunny disposition."

Cole's soft southern draw had taken on an edge that told Faith he wasn't kidding. Evidently, Jimmy noticed it as well. As he dropped the keys into Cole's palm, they jingled noisily, making Lizzie stir and whine in her sleep.

"Better not loosh them," he warned Cole. The man's body rocked back and forth, while his watery eyes squinted in an effort to focus.

"Of the many times I've taken your keys, have I ever lost them?"

Jimmy considered the question for moment and then shook his head, the movement causing him to sway precariously against the car. "Nah."

Cole tucked the keys in his shirt pocket. "I'll leave them at the office. You can come by for them on your way to work tomorrow morning."

Jimmy nodded drunkenly and then staggered toward Keeler's Market, mumbling something about uppity women and pushy lawmen, and a man needing a drink just to tolerate them.

Not until they were in the car with Lizzie tucked safely in her car seat did Faith allow herself to think about what had just happened. She wasn't use to being protected, and Cole's actions left her with a warm glow she didn't even want to try to acknowledge, but the possibilities sent her into a shocked silence that lasted for most of the ride to her new home.

All her life, people had taken her for granted, taken advantage of her, told her what to do, how to do it, and when she was doing it wrong. And, according to Sloan and her mother, that was all the time. Never, not once, had anyone protected and cared for her and Lizzie as Cole had in the short time since they'd met in Doc Amos' office. Yes, he'd been controlling, but it was a different kind of control, one tempered with caring.

With that realization, came a flash of stark reality. If she allowed Cole past her defenses, she could get very used to it, and she'd sworn never to become reliant on anyone ever again.

Or to fall in love.

Chapter 3

WHEN THEY PULLED into the driveway of the little cottage Doc had allowed Faith and Lizzie to move into, the tightness around Faith's nerves eased. With its beds of rainbow-colored flowers, bright red shutters, and the little front porch complete with a rocking chair to lull Lizzie to sleep, the small, white structure seemed to open its arms to her.

Faith cuddled Lizzie close and entered the building to explore their new home. If the outside made her feel wanted, the interior and its homey country décor personified the word *welcome*. A large braided rug covered the center of the rich oak floor in the small, quaint living room, and cheery yellow tiebacks hung at the windows. An arrangement of silk daisies graced the coffee table.

She continued to explore her new home. The kitchen was small but friendly. Bright rays of sunshine coming through the three windows above the sink washed the kitchen with golden sunlight. Through one of the windows she could see another house peeking through the trees. For a moment, she wondered who her neighbor was. After searching her memory of the town and its layout, she realized that the house belonged to Lydia and George Collins, the mayor of Carson and his wife.

The idea of having someone close by pleased her. However, if she remembered correctly, Lydia would be more help in an emergency than her husband. Faith turned from the windows to look around the kitchen. She spotted the large pantry and chuckled. The few things she'd bought at Keeler's Market would barely fill the shelves.

Footsteps behind her drew her attention to the doorway. Cole entered with his arms full of grocery bags. "I'll check the attic for that crib." Cole deposited the groceries on the counter.

"Thanks." She looked down at her drowsy-eyed daughter cuddled into her shoulder. "I think Lizzie's ready for bed."

Once Cole had dragged the crib down from the attic and set it up in the smaller of the two bedrooms, Faith put Lizzie and her teddy bear down for a nap. Lizzie snuggled close to her constant companion and closed her eyes. Faith breathed a sigh of contentment. Maybe this wasn't going to be so bad after all.

As she reentered the living room, she was surprised to find Cole still there. For some reason, she'd expected him to be gone. He rose from the sofa and grinned at her. "I turned on the electric and the water, but I thought I'd stick around to make sure there's nothing else I can do for you before I leave."

His smile warmed her down to the soles of her sneakers . . . and she hated that it did. The sooner she got him out of here, the better she'd feel. "I think that's it. Thanks for your help."

He picked up his hat from the sofa. "I left my phone number on the kitchen table. If you find there is something you need, just give me a call."

Why didn't he just go?

She couldn't look at him. His eyes held too much kindness, too much understanding, too much . . . Faith glanced into the tiny kitchen. "Thanks, but you're forgetting that I don't have a phone."

"Cell phone?"

She shook her head.

"You and the little one out here with no phone? Not good."

"Well, until I get a job, I'll have to hope I don't need one."

Cole thought for a moment, and then took a couple of hesitant steps toward the door. "Well, I guess I'd better get back to the office."

She remained silent, mentally giving him a push that would hurry him from the cottage and, hopefully, from her thoughts.

He took another step, and then turned back to her. "Listen. I've been thinking. I need a housekeeper to clean up around my house for me, do some laundry, and maybe fix my supper." He shook his head. "I'm a lousy cook. I know you need a job. I can't pay you a lot, but it would be enough to feed you and Lizzie until you find something else. How about it?"

Stunned, Faith could only stare at him. Her stomach did a somersault. Work for him? See him every day? Handle his things? She was already fighting an attraction to this handsome man, and putting herself in close proximity to him on a daily basis wouldn't be smart.

Despite her misgivings about putting herself in that kind of situation, she couldn't help but feel gratitude for his concern for her and Lizzie. But when she'd left Atlanta, she'd promised herself that she would take care of herself and her daughter. She'd made the mistake of relying on a man once and . . .

No! She had to stop rehashing the past. It was just that, the past, and she had to concentrate on her future and her daughter's. That left no room for remorse. But there wasn't room for a man either.

"Thanks, but I planned on going job hunting tomorrow. I'm sure I'll find something." *And exactly what do you think you'll find in this little town? You have no qualifications for anything.*

His face melted into an expression of disappointment. "Okay. But the job offer stands if you need it."

"Thanks. I really appreciate all you and Doc have done for me . . . for us. But it's time I started doing for myself."

Cole frowned and opened the door. "I'll see you around, Faith."

"Goodbye, Sheriff." Her stilted farewell rang with finality.

He paused for a moment, nodded, and then he was gone.

With his departure, it felt as if all the air had been sucked from the room.

THE NEXT MORNING, Faith hitched Lizzie a little higher on her hip. She'd only been walking toward town for a short time, and already her blouse and Lizzie's pink sundress were soaked with perspiration. Even the fur on Lizzie's bear was matted and wet. Sweat poured down Faith's back and temples. The straps of the tote bag holding a drink for Lizzie and a few other necessities bit deeply into her shoulder.

Faith hadn't remembered this walk into town being this long, but then again, she'd never made it while carrying a child. She'd considered allowing Lizzie to walk, but the way the cars passing them didn't seem to slow down, she'd decided against it. As she trudged along, and the sun's rays seemed to get hotter with every step, she began to wonder how smart this idea had been. But what other alternative did she have? There was no one to take care of Lizzie so she could walk the distance alone. She had no means of transportation. No way to call someone to drive her. Even if she'd had a phone, who would she call? Certainly not her judgmental mother. And most definitely not the helpful sheriff.

The unseasonably warm late spring day and the burdens of life settled on her already bowed shoulders. Would she make it through this? Was she wise to have come back here where the job opportunities were so limited?

"Stop it!" she scolded. "You can do this. You're strong." Lizzie squirmed in her arms, reminding her of her responsibility to this small life. "You *have* to do this."

The sound of another approaching car broke the woodsy silence. Faith took a deep breath and moved farther onto the side of the road. But rather than pass her, the car slowed and adjusted its speed to her pace. When she looked toward it, she was surprised to see the sheriff's car. Cole was smiling at her through the open passenger's side window.

"Need a lift?"

She wanted to say no, but one look at Lizzie's flushed cheeks and sweat-soaked curls changed her mind. "That would be great. Thanks."

Cole pulled the car to the shoulder of the road in front of her, stopped it, climbed out, and opened the trunk to reveal the child's car seat he'd used for Lizzie the day before. After reinstalling the seat, he scooped Lizzie from Faith's arms and buckled the little girl and her bear in while Faith collapsed in the passenger seat.

"Where are you going?" Cole asked as he slipped behind the wheel, closed the car door and cranked up the AC.

Why did he have to be so considerate? Why was she allowing him to unnerve her? Too hot and exhausted to think about anything but how good it felt to get off her feet, Faith leaned back. As the cool air bathed her face and shoulders, she sighed. "To town. I need to find a job."

"You could have asked me to pick you up when I was at your house yesterday." Cole pulled the car onto the road. "It wouldn't have been a problem. I come this way every day." He glanced in the rearview mirror. "Lizzie shouldn't be out in this heat."

Guilt washed over Faith. He was right, of course. But she wasn't about to tell him that. "I didn't want to bother anyone." She avoided looking at him.

Cole frowned, wondering exactly what she meant. Didn't want to bother anyone or didn't want to be in his company? She'd made it quite clear yesterday that she didn't want anything from him. But he had a gut feeling it was more than that.

They rode in silence for a while until he couldn't stand it any longer. "So where did you plan to look for a job?"

Faith shrugged. "I don't know. I guess I'll start at the Terri's Tea Room."

The deafening silence engulfed them again.

"My offer to work for me still stands," he finally said, hoping she'd changed her mind. He wanted very much to help her, but evidently her pride made that very difficult. He couldn't force her to take the job.

When she didn't reply, he glanced in her direction, and, taking into account the way she was staring out the side window, he guessed no answer to his job offer reminder would be forthcoming from her.

Except for Lizzie's incoherent baby babblings coming from the back seat, the rest of the ride proceeded in an uncomfortable silence. Cole wanted to talk Faith into accepting his offer of a job, but she obviously wasn't into making conversation of any kind, especially if it included working for him. Still, he wanted to press the subject, but if he hadn't learned anything else from his defunct former relationship, he'd learned that wanting something and pushing for acceptance didn't necessarily mean you'd get it. Sometimes what you wanted just sent the other person running in the opposite direction. Like it had with Diane.

The large white sign sporting an ornate teapot and the words Terri's Tea Room dragged him from his thoughts.

"Here we are," he announced unnecessarily.

Cole pulled the squad car to the curb, jumped out, retrieved Lizzie and her faithful teddy bear from the backseat, and handed the child to Faith. "Let me know when you're ready to go home, and I'll pick you up. I'll be at the office." When she opened her mouth, he was certain she was about to protest, but he stopped her with a raised palm. "It's not up for discussion." He hated himself for using Lizzie, but he knew it was the only thing to stop Faith's argument. "Lizzie can't tolerate this heat, and by the time you're ready to go home, she'll be wiped out and cranky."

"Thanks." As though she wanted to say more, she paused for only a moment, but then turned toward the building and walked away.

IT WAS NEARLY two o'clock, and the tearoom held just a handful of patrons.

Faith spotted Terri Medford, the owner, sitting at a table near the window talking to an older woman that Faith instantly recognized as Granny Jo Hawks. Not wanting to interrupt their conversation, she hung back.

Granny Jo leaned past Terri and smiled at Faith. "Faith Chambers, is that you, dear?"

"Yes, ma'am." Faith still hung back.

Terri turned to see who Granny was talking to and waved Faith over. "Come and join us. We're just passing the time of day." She stood. "I'll get something for the little one to sit on." She hurried off toward the kitchen and returned quickly with a pink plastic booster seat in one hand and a stack of cellophane-wrapped saltines in the other. "The kids always like a cracker."

Faith remembered Terri. She looked much the same as she

had when Faith used to come here after school with her friends for a soda before going home. The only differences in Terri's appearance were the smatterings of gray scattered through her ebony hair and maybe a few more faint wrinkles. Otherwise, she was the same sweet-natured woman who'd greeted every customer with a warm welcome and a smile that made her green eyes twinkle.

Faith placed Lizzie in the booster seat and slid her up to the table. Terri unwrapped a cracker and handed it to Lizzie. She grabbed it and began gnawing on it immediately. Once Faith had her daughter settled, she slid into the only empty chair at the table.

Terri remained standing. "Can I get you something, dear? Coffee? Pop? Sweet tea?"

"Nothing for me, thanks. Actually, I didn't come here to eat."

"Oh?" Terri sat down and grinned at Faith.

Faith gathered her courage around her and took a deep breath. "I need a job."

The smile on the woman's face crumbled. Genuine regret took its place. She covered Faith's hand with her own. "I'm so sorry darlin', but business hasn't been all that good lately. Everyone in Carson is off on vacations and such. There's barely enough business to keep my one waitress busy. I'm not sure when I'll be taking anyone on again."

Disappointment flooded Faith. "Do you happen to know of anyone in town who's looking for help?" She failed miserably at keeping the desperation out of her voice.

Granny Jo and Terri exchanged glances. "No, I'm afraid I don't." Terri stood again. "Have you and this little sweetie had lunch?" Faith shook her head. "Well, Granny and I were just about to eat, and we'd love it if you'd join us."

Faith straightened, her thoughts going to the few dollars in her purse, money she couldn't afford to squander on the luxury of lunch. To that end, she'd packed a couple of sandwiches for her and Lizzie in her tote bag along with some fruit to eat on the bench in the square. "I . . . uh . . . I don't—"

Terri stopped her with a hand to her arm. "My treat. And I won't take no for an answer." Then she hurried away again.

Hating that she must have looked like she needed Terri's charity, Faith kept her gaze centered on Lizzie as she devoured her third cracker.

Suddenly, a warm hand cupped her chin and gently raised it until she was eye-to-eye with Granny Jo. "There's no shame in letting folks lend a hand through the hard times. You should know that's the way of things here in Carson. We help our own."

Too choked up to speak, Faith nodded and forced a smile. Granny Jo's protective concern surrounded Faith like a warm blanket, reminding her of her beloved Gramma Harrison, her maternal grandmother. Mentally, she pulled the emotional blanket Granny Jo offered tightly around her. Maybe coming home hadn't been a mistake. Maybe, with the love and help of these gentle people, this could be a new start for her and Lizzie.

The compassion of this small community seemed to reach out to her from every corner. Now, all she had to do was find a way to support her little family, and that prospect was looking dimmer every day.

Chapter 4

FAITH HAD CHOKED down the hamburger and fries that she'd been served by Terri's waitress. Lizzie had devoured the cut-up hot dog Terri had brought her. Getting the food past the clog of fear and disappointment in her throat had been hard, but Faith didn't want to insult Terri's generosity by not eating.

Faith glanced at Lizzie. Her nap time had come and gone and the little girl's eyes drooped. She flashed a lazy smile at her mother, then yawned, laid her head on her teddy bear and rubbed her eyes.

When Terri left the table to take their dirty dishes to the kitchen and get Lizzie a dish of ice cream for dessert, Granny Jo covered Faith's cold hand with hers. Without thinking, Faith turned her hand over and clasped Granny Jo's. The warmth emanating from the older woman's hand seeped into Faith, clearing away some of the almost paralyzing fear of being on her own with a small child and no immediate prospects for a means of support.

"It appears like that little one needs a nap?"

Faith nodded. She knew Lizzie should be home in her crib sleeping, but Faith had to consider her priorities, and finding a job was at the top of her to-do list. "I know, but unfortunately, I have no one to watch her while I job hunt, so she has to come with me."

Granny Jo squeezed her hand and flashed a knowing smile. "Well, you do now. You tell me what time tomorrow, and I'll be there with bells on."

Faith shook her head. "Oh, I couldn't ask you to do that. Besides, I can't pay you."

"Did I say anything about money?" Granny Jo frowned. "Goodness, I'll do it just to spend some time with that little sweetheart. For me, that's payment enough."

Gratitude flooded Faith. Tears burned her eyes. She wasn't sure she'd ever get used to the benevolence of the goodhearted people of Carson. "Thank you, Granny Jo."

It was becoming harder and harder to stick to her vow of independence and not depend on anyone else for her and Lizzie's well-being. Besides, considering she'd accepted a house and groceries from Doc Amos, transportation from Cole, and lunch from Terri, Faith decided that ship had already sailed.

GRANNY JO HAD offered to take Faith and Lizzie home, but Faith had declined for a couple of reasons. She was determined to hit every store on Main Street in hopes of finding work. Besides, Granny didn't have a car seat for Lizzie.

However, by the time Faith had carried a sleeping baby's dead weight up and down the street and been turned down by all the shopkeepers, she wished she'd accepted Granny's offer of a ride. She knew she couldn't walk home while carrying Lizzie, and that left her one alternative . . . Cole Ainsley.

After shifting her sleeping daughter to a more comfortable position on her hip, Faith crossed the street and reluctantly headed toward the sheriff's office. By the time she stepped through the door and into the office, putting one foot in front of the other took concentrated effort.

The man at the desk, who Faith recognized immediately as Laureene Talbot's husband Graylin, looked up from what he'd been doing. "Yes, ma'am, can I help you?"

"I need to see Sheriff Ainsley." Her voice betrayed her fatigue. She swayed on her feet.

Deputy Talbot shot from his chair and rounded the desk. "Why don't you sit down here, and I'll get the sheriff." He guided her to a straight-backed chair against the wall.

Faith sank into it gratefully and positioned Lizzie on her lap. "Thank you."

The deputy nodded and then hurried off down a side hall. Moments later, he returned trailing behind Cole.

"Are you okay?" Cole kneeled down in front of her. Her obvious exhaustion tore at his heart.

Without any resistance from Faith, he lifted Lizzie from her arms. The child's clothing was damp with perspiration and a dark sweat stain showed on the front of Faith's blouse. Deep blue circles beneath her eyes showed vividly against her creamy skin. The worry lines he'd seen on her face the first day he'd met her seemed to have deepened. From her defeated expression, he guessed that her job hunt had been a flop.

Placing his free hand under her elbow, he pulled her to her feet. "Let's get you two home." As he guided Faith toward the door, he paused and turned to Graylin. "Watch the store. I'll be back in a bit."

Graylin gave his boss a sharp salute. "Yes, sir."

Under other circumstances, Cole would have explained to Graylin, again, that he did not have to salute him, but at the moment, that was the least of his worries. Getting Lizzie and Faith home topped his to-do list.

He slid his arm around Faith's shoulders and hurried her from the office. Lizzie snuggled into the crook of his neck and closed her eyes. He inhaled her baby scent and allowed a new contentment to wash over him.

As soon as that soft, sweet smell filled his nostrils, the familiar dreams of a family took shape in his head. He quickly pushed them aside. No sense starting something he couldn't finish. Faith had made it clear that she wasn't interested, and he wouldn't be in Carson long enough to put down roots. As soon as the election was held and a new sheriff took office, he'd be gone.

Oddly, that didn't feel as satisfying as it once had. And if he wasn't planning on settling in Carson, why the heck was he so determined to get Faith to work for him? He liked to think it was because he wanted to see her self-sufficient. But, deep down, he knew there was more to it than that. Much more. And much more selfish.

He settled Lizzie in her car seat and then opened the car door for Faith. Just then, a car slowed to a crawl as it passed them. Faith stared at the driver.

"You know her?"

Faith nodded. "I'd recognized that condemning glare anywhere. It's my mother."

FAITH JOLTED AWAKE. She sat up and looked around, amazed that the car had come to a stop, and that they were parked in her driveway. Embarrassed that she'd fallen asleep, she quickly climbed from the car without looking at Cole and hurried around to the other side to get her daughter. When she got there, Faith found Cole already holding the little girl, who had snuggled up against his wide shoulder and gone back to sleep.

When she reached for her daughter, Cole shook his head. "I'll take her."

Apprehension sliced through her. If he carried Lizzie, he'd have to come inside. She didn't want him in her house again. She wasn't exactly sure why, but . . . "No need. I can handle her."

He frowned. "That wasn't a question, Faith. You're dead on your feet. I'll carry Lizzie." He walked around her and headed for the house, leaving her with little choice but to follow.

She had to admit he was right. She was exhausted. But that had nothing to do with her not wanting him inside. So why was it she was trying to keep him out of her home? Out of her life? Was it really because she resented him doing things for her?

That couldn't be it. She'd been selling herself on that excuse ever since she'd met Cole, but now, she wasn't so sure. After all, she'd allowed so many people to help: Doc and Harriet Amos, Granny Jo, Terri. So what was it about Cole Ainsley that made her take a step back from his kindness while she willing accepted it from others?

Faith pushed her dilemma aside. She was far too tired to think.

Inside, Cole went directly to the bedroom where he'd set up the crib the day before. Faith headed for the kitchen, knowing if she didn't start supper before sitting down to rest, she might never get up, and neither she nor Lizzie would eat. She opened the refrigerator and surveyed her choices for supper.

"Not a good idea." Faith jumped. She spun around to find Cole behind her pushing the basement door closed. "You have an inquisitive little girl who could fall down those basement stairs."

Faith shook her head. "I didn't leave that open." She frowned and leaned against the refrigerator. "At least I don't think I did." Her tired brain refused to work. She shrugged it off.

Cole stared at her for a moment, and then guided her to a kitchen chair. "Sit. Lizzie was stirring when I laid her down and will no doubt be looking for supper in a few minutes. You sit there, and I'll warm up some soup for you."

It took all her strength, but Faith sprang to her feet. "Stop it! I'm fine. I can take care of it," she snapped.

Cole opened his mouth, no doubt to argue the point, but appeared to think better of it. "Okay," he finally said. "Listen. I'm a cop. I'm trained to step in and help where I see it's necessary. I'm not trying to run your life. Just help you out. Okay?"

She nodded.

"I'll pick you up tomorrow morning. Is that okay?"

She nodded again. Before she could add that she was grateful for him going out of his way, he was heading for the door.

She watched him leave and immediately regretted her sharp tone of voice. He was just trying to make her life easier. Once again, she wondered why she couldn't accept Cole's benevolence. Was it because he sometimes got a bit heavy-handed, sometimes a little smothering? Or was it something else? Something her heart was trying to tell her.

FAITH HAD JUST brought Lizzie into the kitchen the next morning and set her on the floor with a few toys when there was a knock on the back door. She had no idea who it could be. Only Doc, Harriet, and Cole knew she was there. Besides, he always came to the front door. For a moment, her heart pounded with an old and familiar fear. Then she reminded herself that Sloan was dead and no longer had any claim on her or Lizzie.

Faith picked up Lizzie, then cautiously peeked through the glass in the door and spotted a young boy, of about ten or eleven, and his rather shaggy, gray dog staring up at her. The boy flashed a wide smile and called "Hello" to her.

She returned his smile and swung the door open. "Hello."

Warm brown eyes sparkled up at her. "I'm Davy Collins and this here's," he pointed at the dog, "Sadie. We live next door, and my mom said we needed to come over and be neighborly." He grinned again, but this time, it seemed to cover his entire face and exposed a missing tooth.

"Well, hello, Davy. I'm Faith and this," she pointed at her daughter, "is my little girl, Lizzie. Would you like to come in?"

"Sure. Can Sadie come, too?"

Faith stared at the dog. It was very big and sent a chill of apprehension down her spine. She clutched Lizzie a little closer.

The child squealed and pointed at the dog. "Dawg!"

Faith tightened her hold on the squirming child. "Is . . . it friendly?"

He turned to his dog. "Oh, she sure is, ma'am." He gave the dog's ear a gentle tug. "Aren't you, girl?" The dog turned to Davy and licked his hand.

Still a bit anxious, Faith relented, but held tight to Lizzie. "Okay, bring her in."

"Come on, Sadie." They ambled past Faith and into the kitchen.

Sadie immediately walked to Faith's side and smelled Lizzie's bare toes and then licked the bottom of her foot. The child giggled and pulled her foot out of Sadie's reach. The shaggy dog's tail beat happily against the side of the cabinet.

"Your dog likes children."

The boy laughed, and then said matter-of-factly, "Lots of folks think Sadie's a dog, but she's a wolf."

Wolf?

Faith's blood turned to ice in her veins. Her body remained

frozen in place despite her desire to run to another room and barricade herself and Lizzie behind a closed door.

"It's okay. Don't be afraid. Sadie is really tame. She likes people, and she's never hurt anybody." Davy patted the wolf's head. "My dad doesn't believe that, but since he and Mom got divorced, she says he doesn't have any say anymore."

Barely registering that the mayor and his wife were no longer together, Faith continued to eye the large wolf. Not about to tempt fate, she continued to hold on to Lizzie, who was now squirming to get down.

"She 'specially likes little kids, so you can let Lizzie down." When Faith made no move to release Lizzie, he shrugged. "Anyway, my mom says you should come over for coffee when you can. Lizzie can see Sadie's puppies, too. She's got three babies. My mom says she thinks Sadie got cozy with our neighbor's German Shepherd." He grinned and cupped his mouth with his hand. "Getting cozy means they had sex."

Faith coughed. "Well, I'll take your mom up on her offer of coffee first chance I get. Please tell her thank you for me."

"Okay. I gotta go to work now." Davy moved to the door. "I help Doc Mackenzie out at the animal hospital. Come on, Sadie." He motioned to the wolf. She immediately went to his side. He waved goodbye, and they left.

Faith breathed a sigh of relief. She couldn't believe she'd just had a wolf in her kitchen. Lord, but life in Carson was a lot more exciting than she remembered it. She set Lizzie on the floor and piled her blocks in front of her.

"You stay there while mommy makes coffee," she told the toddler. Cole would be there soon to pick her up. The realization brought a strange bottomless sensation to the pit of her stomach. Yes. Definitely. Coffee was what she needed to combat the sheriff's charm. Although, she wasn't sure that a stiff shot of Scotch might be more effective at putting to rest her unwelcome attraction to the handsome Cole Ainsley, except alcohol usually made her more romantic. She'd stick with coffee.

Chapter 5

WHEN SHE HEARD the sound of a car's engine, Faith froze. Cole. A wave of apprehension gripped her, followed quickly by the acceleration of her heartbeat.

She hit the brew button on the coffeemaker and then hurried to the living room to look out the window. Relief washed over her when Granny Jo climbed from the car carrying a small box. Granny was keeping her promise to stop by today and babysit Lizzie while she went to town to look for a job again.

Faith had expected Cole to be the one in her driveway, since he'd told her he'd pick her up the day before. Although she was grateful, she wished she didn't have to depend on him for transportation, but she saw no way around it. Unfortunately, she had no car and borrowing one was out of the question. Faith had never gotten her driver's license.

She sighed. Fighting her growing attraction for the handsome sheriff was exhausting her and complicating her life when she didn't need any more problems. She didn't have the extra energy to expend on it right now. Taking care of Lizzie, finding a job, and keeping her financial head above water had her tied in knots.

Opening the front door, she smiled at Granny Jo. "Good morning. Come on in. A fresh pot of coffee is almost made and waiting in the kitchen."

"Good morning, dear." Granny held out the box. "Here's some cookies for you and that sweet daughter of yours." She gave Faith the box she'd carried from the car.

The aroma emanating from it made Faith's mouth water. Homemade, chocolate chip cookies. A treat she hadn't had in a very long time. Gramma Harrison had been a wonderful baker. Faith had often hurried to her home after school to indulge in one of her grandmother's baked treats—one thing on a very short list of things Faith missed about her childhood. Those things she did miss were always connected to her loving grandmother.

"And I'd be mighty grateful for a cup of that coffee." Granny Jo's voice roused Faith from her thoughts.

They made their way to the kitchen, and Granny took a seat near where Lizzie was playing on the floor. Faith poured two cups and placed them on the table, then added spoons, sugar, and a creamer. She sat across from Granny, added sugar to her cup, and nervously stirred her coffee, waiting for what she knew would be the inevitable question—*why had she come home?*

Her movements halted when Granny laid her hand on Faith's. Then, as if the older woman had read her mind, Granny Jo said, "Honey, relax. If you're worried that I'm going to start cross-examining you about your reasons for coming back to Carson, don't. I've learned over the years that when a body's ready to talk, they will. No need to push them."

Faith smiled. Her whole body relaxed. She wasn't ready to talk about Sloan having been into something illegal and what had gone wrong with her "dream" life in the big city. Maybe she just didn't want to face her failure. Maybe she wanted to avoid the embarrassment of admitting she had questionable taste in men. Maybe it was because she wanted more than anything to erase any memories of her time in Atlanta, and talking about it just brought it all back to life. Whatever the reason, that Granny was not expecting Faith to talk about it made her whole body relax.

"I will say this, and you can take it for what you will." Granny squeezed her hand. "Sometimes you have to stop looking for the happily ever after and be happy after all." Granny sipped her coffee, and then set the cup carefully on the table. "Over the years, I've learned that today and yesterday might not be the best, but there's always tomorrow."

That might sound good and even look good on paper, but Faith had learned from Sloan's half-baked promises not to plan too far into the future. She'd long ago lost any reliance on the promise of a tomorrow.

AS COLE DROVE toward Faith's house, he again questioned his motivation for inserting himself into her life. It wasn't as if he had a future in Carson.

Coming here and taking the job had just been a favor for his father. When he'd had a heart scare, the old man had finally realized he was too old to be playing cops and robbers—not that Carson's crime rate was all that high—and had moved himself and his wife to Florida. But not before he'd guilted Cole into taking over as sheriff until his elected term ended. After that, Cole would be free to pursue a new life far from Carson.

So what was the answer to his quandary? Was he just trying to be the Good Samaritan? Or was there more to it? Was he looking for a family? Was he interested in Faith for a completely emotional reason?

A sudden vision of the woman in question raced through his mind, followed by a vision of Lizzie with red lollipop juice dribbling down her chin and onto the fur of her faithful teddy bear. That old longing for a family reared its ugly head. That had to be the answer. His desire for children, for a family, had blurred his reasoning. If that were true, he had to stop it right now before it got out of hand. It wouldn't be fair to start something with her knowing he would be leaving soon.

"Get a grip, Ainsley. She's made it perfectly clear that she doesn't want your help. Take her into town today and home tonight, and then be done with her."

He pulled the squad car into Faith's driveway and parked beside an old, blue Ford he recognized as Granny Jo Hawks's cherished vehicle. Word was that the car had been Earl's, and she refused to get rid of it no matter how rundown it became.

Cole climbed from the squad car and walked to the front porch. For a moment, he stood there, renewing his vow to keep his emotions in check. But when the door opened and he gazed into Faith's beautiful face, all his good intentions flew out the window. Plain and simple, the woman took his breath away.

"Morning, Faith," he finally managed.

"Hi, Cole." She looked as hesitant as he felt. "Come on in. I have to get my purse." She stepped to the side to allow him to pass, and the smell of her flowery perfume wafted up to him, further scrambling his brain.

"Morning, Cole," Granny called from the kitchen. She was building a tower out of Lizzie's blocks and then laughed when the child knocked it down.

"Granny." Trying not to look at Faith as she collected her purse and kissed Lizzie goodbye, he touched the brim of his hat. But he caught himself following her movements as closely as a cat stalking a mouse. When she turned toward him, he blinked, as though waking from a dream, and quickly averted his gaze. "Well, we should be going."

Faith tucked a strand of hair behind her ear, smiled nervously, and nodded. "Okay. Bye, Lizzie." She waved at the baby, who was intent on knocking down the block tower again. "I shouldn't be long, Granny."

"Take as long as you need, dear. Miss Lizzie and I have a lot of playing to get in today. Good luck." Then she winked at Cole.

Why was she wishing him good luck?

COLE AND FAITH had ridden for about a mile in total silence. Finally, he broke the ice. "So, where will you be going today to look for work?"

"Granny said that her granddaughter, Becky, might need help at the social service office. She wasn't sure about it, but I figure it couldn't hurt to ask." Faith swallowed hard, trying to remove the instant feeling of contentment that overcame her every time she heard his velvety, deep voice.

Keeping his gaze on the road, he nodded. "That's a possibility. But what if that doesn't work out for you?"

Was he going around the barn to get back to his offer of a job? "I'll have to keep looking. I can't just give up. I have Lizzie to think about."

She went silent, waiting for him to renew the offer, but it didn't come. Had he given up? While the idea pleased her because she wouldn't have to find an excuse to turn him down again, at the same time, she felt a distinct stab of disappointment that he'd caved so easily.

What was wrong with her? Either she wanted this man in her life or she didn't. This wasn't rocket science. So why was she playing mental games with herself?

Trust.

The word jumped into her mind like a boulder rolling off a cliff and hitting the ground below with a loud *thud*. She didn't trust Cole. But to be fair, it wasn't just him she distrusted. It was all men. Her father had stood to the side and allowed her mother to browbeat Faith with religion, and Sloan had made promises he never kept. Why should she trust any man ever again?

The car stopping drew her out of her thoughts.

"Here you are," Cole said. He smiled, but she felt like the gesture was more forced than spontaneous. Despite that, it still had the power to make her breath catch in her throat. "Good luck."

"Thanks." Faith climbed from the car and closed the door. She watched as he drove away from the curb and went down the street toward the sheriff's office.

FAITH WALKED confidently into the building housing the social services offices. She and Becky Hawks, Hart now, had been friends in high school, so Faith felt fairly at ease asking her for a job. However, she'd make it very clear it had nothing to do with their friendship.

When she entered the office, Becky was talking to another woman at a desk in the front of the room. "Becky?"

Becky straightened and turned toward her. She stared at Faith for a moment, and then her expression changed from confusion to recognition. "Faith? Faith Chambers? I can't believe it's you. Granny said you were back in town."

"Hi, Becks."

She rushed forward and enveloped Faith in a bear hug. Becky released her, and then guided her to an inner office. "It's been so long since I last saw you. How are you? What have you been doing? Where are you living?" Then she stopped talking, shook her head, and laughed. Then, encumbered by an obviously advanced pregnancy, she seated herself behind the desk. "Sorry. I probably should let you answer one question at a time. It's just that I'm so happy to see you."

Faith sat in a black vinyl chair facing Becky.

"So how are you?"

"Fine." Faith was aware that her voice was shaky and without much conviction, but she hoped that her elevated chin might say otherwise. The last thing she wanted was to appear like a pathetic waif.

Becky frowned. "Why don't I believe that?" She leaned her forearms on the desk and looked Faith in the eye. "Remember, we used to tell each other everything? So come on, girl, spill it."

Just like her grandmother, Becky saw right through Faith's flimsy attempt at confidence. She sighed. "I need a job. Granny told me you might have something." Faith took a deep breath. "I'm not trained for much, but I can do filing and cleaning up around here, and—"

"Wait." Becky held up her hand. Her expression told Faith this was not going to be good news. Disappointment filled her. "I'm sorry, Faith, but I don't have any openings. This is a very small satellite office and our funding isn't geared to pay for any more employees than Mandy and me."

Faith's friend looked truly regretful, but her remorse didn't help dissolve the growing lump of desperation in Faith's stomach. This was her last hope. Well, not her *last* hope. There was the job Cole had offered her. The desperation grew to the size of a basketball.

Chapter 6

BY THE TIME Faith left Becky's office, all she had to show for the day was a promise from her friend to let her know if she heard about anyone hiring and a bigger ball of desperation weighing down her stomach. Her employment prospects had just gone from dim to jet black.

She walked across the street to Terri's Tea Room. Though she was counting pennies, she decided she needed a cup of coffee and some time alone to think about where she'd go from here.

The waitress appeared moments after Faith found a seat close to the front window. "What can I get you?"

"Coffee, please." The young girl smiled and disappeared, only to return quickly with a steaming cup of coffee. Faith added sugar and stirred while she gazed out on Main Street.

Her hand closed automatically around the one possession she'd always found comfort in—the locket her grandmother had given Faith just before she died. She recalled Gramma's words as if she could hear her speaking them into her ear. "Baby girl, hang on to this because it holds the answers to all your tomorrows."

Faith looked down at the treasured piece of jewelry. The sun glinted off her ruby birthstone set in the middle of a gold rose on the face of the locket. "If only that were true, Gramma." Even if she pawned it, which she refused to even consider, she'd get so little for it that it wouldn't help her financially for long. She dropped the locket back inside the neckline of her blouse.

While she sipped the aromatic coffee, she scanned the street for somewhere she hadn't gone on her job search. But as she her gaze moved from store to store, she realized her options had run dry. Well, not completely dry. There was one job open to her . . . keeping house for Cole.

The more she thought about it, the less intimidating it seemed. After all, she'd be there while he was at work, so her fears of what would happen if she was exposed to his charms for too long were unfounded. She could do it. What's more, she had no choice. She must do it.

Faith finished her coffee, and then used the phone behind the tearoom's desk to call the sheriff's office to let Cole know she was ready to go home. When Graylin told her Cole had been called out of the office and it might be about a half an hour before he could pick her up, she went back to her table and ordered another coffee.

Though she still had some reservations about working for Cole, the idea that she had a job in her future relieved some of the knots in her stomach, and she was able to relax a bit. Though she suspected the job offer from Cole was more a benevolent gesture than because he needed a housekeeper, she'd give it her all. She'd always been a good worker and earned every penny of her wages. This job would be no different.

A half hour later, she left the tearoom and positioned herself on the bench outside. She glanced down Main Street and noticed a familiar silver car coming her way. As it got closer, it slowed. For the second time, her mother stared at her, shook her head, and then accelerated down the street. Faith cringed. It had been inevitable that in a small town like Carson she would run into one or both of her parents eventually. She had, however, hoped it would be later.

But she'd barely had time to think about it when a black and white squad car pulled up in front of her. The passenger door swung opened, and Cole flashed that devastating smile at her. "Any luck?" he asked as she climbed into the front seat.

"No. Becky only has enough funding for two employees. Since she already has Mandy Michaels working for her, she doesn't have any other openings." Faith went silent.

"I'm sorry it didn't work out for you." His voice dripped with sincerity. "I hope I didn't take too long. Granny Jo called me to borrow my baby car seat. Seems Becky's little one got hurt at nursery school, and she needed Granny to go to their house to watch him. She took Lizzie with her."

"Oh. I hope he's okay." Suddenly, Faith sat up straight and stared at him. "How will I get Lizzie home?"

"Don't worry. I'll go pick her up after I drop you off. If that's okay with you. It's just that you look beat."

She was about to protest, but he was right. She was exhausted and wasn't looking forward to the ride up the mountain. But, she'd only known this man for a few days. Could she let him pick up her daughter? She glanced sideways at his profile and realized her trepidation was ridiculous. He'd already proven how much he cared for Lizzie. She leaned back, knowing Lizzie would be taken care of by both Granny and Cole.

They rode in silence for a while. The deserted road made travel easy. The only other car they saw was a white SUV parked on the side of the road. A breakdown no doubt. Since no one stood near the car, Faith assumed they'd walked the mile to town for help. Recalling her walk yesterday, a wave of sympathy for the car's driver washed over her.

Cole cast a casual quick glance at the car. "Out of towner."

She frowned. "How do you know that?"

He smiled. "Georgia plate."

Feeling a bit foolish, she didn't reply. Instead, she stared out the passenger side window at the passing scenery. Realizing her preoccupation with the sights around her was nothing more than a way to put off the inevitable, Faith swung around in the seat to face him and took a deep fortifying breath. "Cole?"

"Yes."

"I've been thinking." She paused for another breath. "If it's still available, I'll take your job offer."

"Good."

She didn't like the satisfied smile that accompanied his one-word reply. Had he set a trap that she'd just sprung it with herself in it?

COLE DROPPED FAITH off and left to pick up Lizzie at Becky's house. Faith went to her bedroom, kicked off her shoes, and changed into more comfortable clothes. After throwing her discarded clothes in the hamper, she headed to the kitchen to start the coffeemaker. The least she could do after all the running around he'd been doing for her was to offer Cole a cup of hot coffee when he got back. Once the coffee was brewing, she scanned the refrigerator for something for supper.

As she walked from the bedroom and into through the living room, she came to a sudden stop.

"What the—"

Books littered the floor in front of the bookshelf. One of Lizzie's favorite pastimes was to pull the books off the shelf, and, if not caught in time, she would rip the pages out. Since the books came with the house and belonged to Doc Amos and Harriet, Faith kept a close eye on her daughter whenever she was near the shelf. Evidently, Granny Jo had not been as vigilant, but Faith couldn't be upset with her because she hadn't warned her about Lizzie's book-destroying tendencies.

Time later to speculate on how it had happened. First, she had to clean up the mess. Faith picked up the books, checking each for damage and, relieved to find them all intact, she placed them back on the shelf.

"What's going on?"

Cole's voice stopped Faith in the midst of grabbing the last few books and sent that familiar flush to her cheeks. She turned to him. Clutching her teddy bear in one arm and the other arm wrapped around Cole's neck, Lizzie grinned down at her.

"Granny didn't know about my daughter's penchant for books." Faith put the last of the books in its rightful place, then went to Cole and took Lizzie from him, undecided whether to reprimand Lizzie or hug her. Since scolding so long after the transgression seemed nonconstructive, Faith settled for the hug. "Hey, sweet girl." She kissed Lizzie's cheek. "Did you have a nice visit? Are you hungry?"

"Granny said she fed Lizzie supper, so there's no need for you to worry about that."

Lizzie squirmed to get out of her mother's arms. Faith headed into the kitchen and set her daughter on the floor. The child immediately ran to the box Faith had filled with her few toys.

"Thanks for picking her up for me." She tore her gaze away from his and grabbed the coffee carafe. "I was going to make coffee. Do you have time to stay for a cup?"

He smiled, and she felt her knees turn to water. "Coffee would be great." She tried not to watch as he dropped into one of the kitchen chairs. The man would put any woman's heart to pounding, but she had to fight that before she fell into another man's charm-trap.

Thankful for something to do, Faith turned to the task of making a pot of coffee. When the pot was set up and had started emitting gurgling sounds that indicated the brew cycle had started, she busied herself with getting out cups, spoons, sugar, and cream and placing them on the table.

As she worked, she was very aware of Cole's intense gaze following her every movement. Heat radiated through her body. She fought off the feelings. *Just stop it, Faith! You invited the man to stay, so if you didn't want him here, why did you ask him to have coffee with you?* It wasn't that she didn't want Cole here. She did, but at the same time, he scared her. Or was it that she scared herself? No man, not even Sloan, had ever affected her so strongly.

By the time the coffeepot gurgled its last, Faith no longer had an excuse to avoid Cole. She poured two cups of the hot, fragrant brew and carried them to the table.

He sipped at the black liquid and sighed. "This is just what I needed."

That he drank his coffee black didn't surprise her. She'd learned in the brief time she'd known him that Cole didn't seem to have patience for skirting around an issue. The run-in with the town drunk the day she'd arrived in Carson came to mind. He did what he saw as right and made no excuses for it. Oddly, she liked that. If nothing else, she always knew that he cared what happened to her and Lizzie.

He set his cup down and studied her for a moment. "Are you sure you want the job I offered you?"

His question surprised her. "Yes. Why do you ask?"

Cole shrugged. "Well, you didn't seem too eager to take it at first. In fact, I sort of thought you just didn't want to work for me, and then all of a sudden you accepted it."

Faith looked into her cup and stared blankly at the milk bubble floating on the surface. How did she answer this without telling him he was right—that she was afraid of being close to him, afraid she couldn't control her growing attraction to him? That she didn't trust him, but even more important, she didn't trust herself?

"I—" Out of the corner of her eye, she spotted Lizzie about to eat something she'd found on the floor. She jumped up and rushed to her daughter and took away what looked like a piece of dirt. "No, Lizzie. That's yucky." Lizzie's bottom lip protruded and started to quiver. "How about a cookie?"

Faith carried Lizzie to the cabinet and got her one of Granny Jo's cookies, then set her in the highchair next to the table. Cole leaned his chair back on two legs. "So why did you come back here to a little town where you had to know that jobs would be in short supply?"

Good grief! The man went from one impossible question to another. "It was time."

"Why?"

"Why did you come back?" she asked, hoping to turn the tables on him so she wouldn't have to go into the details of her life after leaving Carson.

Cole wasn't stupid. He realized immediately what Faith was up to. But he decided to go along with it . . . for now. Maybe if he opened up to her, he could get her to open up a bit. His gut told him something was bottled up inside her that was poisoning her thinking, and, if he could, he wanted to help her get past it.

He dropped his chair back down on four legs, and then leaned his forearms on the table. "A while back, my dad, Sheriff Ainsley, had a cardiac incident and decided to retire." He grinned. "I have a feeling that my mom had something to do with his decision. So, while she packed for their move to Florida, he called me and asked me to fill out the remainder of his term as sheriff. I had already made plans to leave the Richmond PD, and

I was more than ready for a change of scenery, so I agreed." He held out his hands. "And here I am."

Faith stared at him silently for a moment. "Why don't I believe that's all there was to it? Why were you ready for a change?"

Cole didn't answer immediately. Talking about his breakup with Diane still irritated some tender nerves. But the pain had more to do with his injured pride than with the loss of a loved one. He'd come to realize that he'd loved the idea of starting a family a lot more than he had loved Diane. He'd also come to understand that his incredibly urgent need for a family was in hope of assuaging the horrible effect his job as a homicide detective had on his emotions.

He'd seen too much of the darker side of life. Memories of the wonderful life he'd had as a child had lulled him into believing that a family of his own could erase the images of the horrendous things he'd seen in the line of duty. It was only after Diane left that he'd decided to cut himself off from law enforcement and go into teaching. Unfortunately, his father's health put that plan on the back burner for a while.

"Cole?"

Faith's voice roused him from his memories. He looked into her eyes and saw understanding there, but he still couldn't bring himself to say more. Then she covered his hand with hers and before he knew it, he started talking, and a few minutes later, the entire story was out there in the open.

"And that's my story."

Faith couldn't speak. Her heart ached for this strong, honorable man. Why was life so unfair? All she could think of was how desperately Cole wanted a family while Sloan had thought of her and Lizzie as a burden he had to shoulder, but found easy to ignore. Finally, all she could bring herself to say was, "I'm so sorry."

He shrugged off her sympathy. Then he turned his hand to enclose hers and looked deep into her eyes. "Your turn."

Chapter 7

FAITH STILL WASN'T sure she wanted to bare her past to Cole, but he'd been up front about his, so she took a deep breath and searched for the words to start. "When I graduated from high school, I had lots of dreams that didn't include staying in Carson. As far as I was concerned, this town held nothing but stagnation for me. So, the day after I got my diploma, I packed my bags and bought a bus ticket. I didn't have much money, so I bought one for the largest city I could afford to travel to—Atlanta, Georgia."

Cole nodded. "You're not the first young person who felt that way."

"I'm also not the first young person who made that mistake." Faith smiled ruefully.

"Mistake? How so?"

Cole's prodding niggled Faith, but she also knew that without him pushing her into talking, her story would have ended here. While gathering her thoughts, she brushed the cookie crumbs on Lizzie's highchair tray into a pile. Lizzie immediately swept the pile onto the floor.

"Lizzie!" Faith got up and snatched the broom and dustpan from the broom closet. She swept the crumbs up and deposited them in the trash. "Okay, little girl, it's time for you to get down." She lifted her daughter from the chair and set her and her teddy bear on the floor, then gave her some blocks to play with.

Retaking her seat at the table, she avoided Cole's gaze and sipped at her coffee.

But it didn't deter him. "You were saying?"

The man was relentless. "Where was I?" she asked, stalling again.

"You'd moved to Atlanta," he supplied with a knowing smile.

"Oh, yes. Atlanta." She set the cup down and wrapped her suddenly cold hands around it to absorb the warmth. "I hadn't really thought any of it through, and when I got off the bus in Atlanta, I realized I was almost out of money, with no job prospects, and nowhere to live." Lord, but that sounded so stupid now. No one with half a brain left home without a plan. "I went to a small coffee shop to think about what I'd do next, and I met a man."

Cole sighed and shook his head.

"What?"

"I don't see this ending well."

Faith slumped in the chair. Shame washed over her. "It didn't." She glanced at Lizzie where she sat on the floor totally unaware of the conversation going on above her. "Except for Lizzie. She's the one good thing that came out of my mistakes."

Cole's glance moved to the little girl. "I can't argue that point." He looked back to Faith. "So what happened after you met this man?"

"Nothing good. One thing led to another, and I ended up moving in with him. A few years later, I discovered I was pregnant. It took me almost two years to wise up, but by then, his drug-dealing buddies had killed him. I had Lizzie to think of, and raising her in a big city had never appealed to me, so coming back to Carson was the only thing left for me to do." The memory of the police coming to her door and telling her Sloan had been killed still sent chills chasing over her. Her whole body had begun to shake.

Cole enclosed her hand in his. "Why did they kill him?"

Faith shook her head. The warmth and strength emanating from his hand stopped her trembling. A soothing flood of peace replaced the rekindled fear. "I'm not sure, but I imagine it was over either drugs or money. Sloan made it a point to keep anything he was involved in to himself, but I had my suspicions."

Cole squeezed her hand. "Well, that's all over with. There

are people here who love you and will protect you and your beautiful daughter."

Faith knew he meant he'd protect her, but she didn't believe him. She didn't have the luxury of believing another man and putting her and Lizzie's welfare in his hands.

A streak of late afternoon sunlight shafting through the kitchen window fell across the table between them, separating them as effectively as a brick and mortar wall.

LATER THAT EVENING, Cole looked around his living room and frowned. Having been raised by a mother with a compulsion to put everything where it belonged, and then having served in the Marines for four years, being neat had become second nature to him. His meticulous living room, as well as his entire house, hardly personified the stereotypical single bachelor's living quarters, and definitely not the look of a home that needed a housekeeper.

No used newspapers lay scattered around the homey room. No empty glasses, old beer cans, or dirty plates cluttered the coffee table. The furniture was free of dust. The pine floors glowed with the recent washing and meticulous application of paste wax.

If Faith walked into this room, she would know that he'd created the housekeeping job just for her. Yes, he'd finally admitted to himself that the job was a desperate attempt to gainfully employ Faith. But she wasn't stupid, and now that he'd taken stock of his immaculate dwelling, his ruse might just as well be written in neon across the front of the house.

He stood and scanned the room one more time, then sighed. This had to be one of the craziest things he'd ever done, but . . .

"In for a penny, in for a—whatever that saying is."

Cole picked up the newspaper he'd been reading and systematically scattered the pages over the sofa and floor. After turning his beer can on its side, he grimaced as the remaining contents ran over the coffee table top. He went into the kitchen and removed the dirty supper plates and silverware that he'd carefully placed in the dishwasher. Then he carried them back to the living room and added them to the small beer puddle.

For the next hour, he went through his house leaving a trail of debris behind him. When he'd finished, he looked around and flinched at the mess he'd made. If his mother were here, she'd have a coronary. But if it covered his attempt at fooling Faith, he could live with the mess for one night.

"This better work."

He moved the sports page aside and settled back on the sofa. Suddenly, the pure idiocy of what he'd just done hit him. He began to laugh. The sound echoed through the house. Then a question came to mind, halting the laughter.

Why was he so determined to help this woman that he'd wreck his house? He didn't have to think long about the answer. He'd wanted to help her before, but mainly because of Lizzie. Now, after hearing her story, he was more determined than ever to help Faith, even if she didn't want it. She deserved better. Somehow, he had to prove to her that all men weren't creeps. Some men made promises and kept them. Some men actually protected women and children.

And he knew exactly what he had to do first to help protect Faith and Lizzie.

FAITH RAN OUT of the house and climbed into Cole's car the next morning. Her sneakers were untied, and she nearly fell over the flapping laces. Once in the car and panting, she leaned back, swept her hair from her eyes, and took a breath. As she tied her sneakers, she smiled up at Cole.

"Overslept," was her one word explanation for her breathlessness.

"Where's Lizzie?"

She completed the last bow then sat up. "Granny Jo picked her up about ten minutes ago. When she found out I was going to be cleaning for you today, she knew it would be easier without a two-year-old underfoot, so she volunteered to babysit." She grinned. "I had to agree and gratefully turned Lizzie over to her."

"I thought she didn't have a car seat for Lizzie."

"Evidently Becky had two, so Granny borrowed one. She said she'd bring Lizzie home later. I have to call her from your house before we leave. That is, if you don't mind me using your phone."

Cole started the car, but didn't put it in gear. Instead, he slipped his hand into his pocket and extracted a cell phone. He handed it to Faith. "I want you to have this."

She stared down at it in confusion, and then looked at him. "What—"

"It's a cell phone." He grinned.

She sucked in a breath to quell the instant reaction of her heartbeat to his smile. She turned the phone over in her hand while she got control of her traitorous emotions. When her heart resumed its normal beat and the breathlessness was under control, she turned to him. "I know that. Why are you giving it to me?"

Cole swung around on the seat to face her. He draped an arm casually over the seat. His hand came to rest on her shoulder. She wanted to pull away, but found the touch oddly comforting.

"Because you live out here in the boonies without even a vehicle, and you have a small child. What would you do if Lizzie gets hurt or sick and you need help?" Faith nodded in understanding, a bit ashamed that she hadn't thought of this before. "Your number is taped to the back on a piece of paper. The number below it is my cell. Call me, if you need me." He paused and his expression became serious. "Anytime."

"Okay." She really couldn't afford the luxury of a cell phone, but he was right. On the other hand, she couldn't let him pay for it either. "You can deduct whatever it costs from my pay."

He shook his head. "No need. I have a family plan which allows me to have several phones besides mine on it. My sister's on it, too, and now you. I pay the bill, and it's the same with or without extra phones." He put the car in gear and pulled out of the driveway onto the paved road.

"Cole?"

"Yes." He answered without taking his attention off the road.

"Thanks."

Again, without taking his gaze off the road, he gave a succinct nod.

The man never ceased to amaze her. Other than thanking him whenever he did anything for her, Faith hadn't encouraged him in any way to look after her and Lizzie. Despite that, he continued to do so. In the short time she'd known Cole, he'd done a lot more for her and Lizzie than Sloan had in all the time she'd known him.

She puzzled over this until they reached Cole's house. When he pulled into the driveway, she stared up at the two-story dwelling. If the builder had been in her dreams, he couldn't have come closer to the house she'd always wanted to settle into with her little family.

The morning sun bathed the white paint in brilliance that made it look like a bride on her wedding day. From the twin dormers gracing the roof to the wide porch that wrapped the structure like loving arms, it was absolutely perfect. The only thing missing were two rockers on the front porch.

"It's beautiful, but the front porch needs rocking chairs."

Cole chuckled. "My mother designed it, and my father built it. Neither of them had a clue about designing a house, but they knew what they wanted."

He got out of the car and waited while she got out and rounded the front bumper before leading her up the petunia-lined path and the front stairs, and then opened the door for her.

Faith stepped through the door and into the living room and stopped, her mouth agape. "Oh, my goodness!"

Chapter 8

COLE CLOSED HIS front door behind Faith and looked a bit abashed. "Now you know why I was so desperate to get a housekeeper."

"Uh, yes, I can see that." With her eyes widened in disbelief, Faith continued to survey the totally trashed room. Having lived with Sloan, she knew men weren't always the neatest creatures. Even her father's office had been strewn with books and papers. But this was beyond anything she'd ever witnessed before. "Well, I'd better get started."

Cole left for work shortly after he'd shown her where the cleaning supplies, the vacuum, and the mop and broom were stored. Faith looked around her, wondering where to begin, and settled on starting in the kitchen.

Several exhausting hours later, she flopped down on the sofa to take a break. She sipped at the bottle of icy water she'd retrieved from the fridge. Suddenly, something strange caught her eye. She stood and went to the end table beside the big recliner. Carefully, she ran her fingertips over the wood, and then looked at them. No dust.

How odd that the furniture should be dust free when the rest of the house was a disaster. It didn't make sense that he'd have dusted the furniture and left the rest of the house in such disarray. She went to the window and checked the slats in the blinds. Again, dust free. Then she scanned the brilliantly shining wood floor. This just didn't make sense.

Why would Cole keep everything else immaculate, but clutter the house with discarded clothes, newspapers, and dirty dishes? A sudden suspicion drove her upstairs to his bedroom. Feeling a bit like she was invading his privacy, she swung open the closet doors. Inside, his clothes hung in neat rows. On the floor, his shoes were neatly lined up in pairs.

She moved to his dresser and opened a drawer. Inside, his shirts and sweaters were folded as if he'd just brought them from a store. She opened another drawer. His underwear was rolled and laid out in careful rows, T-shirts folded as skillfully as his sweaters, and his socks joined in matching pairs.

Anger was beginning to build in Faith. She wasn't a pathetic charity case. How dare he treat her like one. Did he think she wouldn't find out that he'd set up the mess she'd spent hours cleaning up? An unexpected pain shot through her heart. She slammed the drawer closed and stomped off to the living room where she'd left the cell phone he'd given her.

She dialed the number on the back and waited. The phone connected after one ring.

"Ainsley."

"Come get me . . . now," she barked into it, then cut off the connection before he could say anything. Then she called Granny Jo and asked her to bring Lizzie home.

COLE RACED TOWARD his house. He had no clue what was going on, but Faith sounded very angry. As he drove, a troubling thought took shape in his mind. Maybe it was his own guilty conscience eating at him, but the reason for Faith's anger was slowly taking shape. She'd figured out what he'd done.

Overhead, dark clouds blocked out the sun and thunder rumbled in the distance. They were in for a summer storm, and from the look of the sky, it was going to be a good one. Something told him that the storm awaiting him would be just as bad.

As he pulled into his driveway, rain began to pelt the windshield of the patrol car. He got out and raced to where Faith waited for him on the porch. As he ran, the rain hit his face, stinging his skin, but he barely felt it. His entire concentration was on the woman on the porch glaring at him with an expression that rivaled the furious sky. The sinking sensation in the pit of his stomach grew as he drew closer to her. He was sure now that she'd figured out his deception.

"Faith, I—"

She threw up her hand in front of him. "Don't. I don't want to hear it. Just take me home." She whipped around him and stepped down off the porch and then strode to the car as though unmindful of the pouring rain.

Cole followed, but before he could get to the car, she'd opened the door and gotten inside, slamming it in his face. For a moment, he stared at her averted face through the rain-speckled glass. He'd expected her to be upset if she figured it out, but not this angry. Rousing himself, he hurried around and got into the driver's seat.

He glanced at her, but she had turned away from him, her posture as stiff as a newly-starched shirt. Rather than try again to explain, he brushed the water from his face and started the car. Obviously, she was in no mood to listen to anything he had to say.

Cole cursed his stupidity all the way to Faith's house. He knew she'd endured lies from Sloan, and yet Cole had tried to deceive her. She must hate him. And with good reason. What he did was thoughtless, dishonest, and self-serving, and he wouldn't blame her if she never trusted a thing he said or did again.

THE SQUAD CAR pulled up outside Faith's house. Eager to be away from Cole, she grabbed the door handle, but his hand on her arm stopped her. "Let me explain."

Visions of Sloan asserting his power over her flashed through her mind. She glared down at Cole's hand, then up at his face. "Let me go."

He released her instantly. She slipped from the car and slammed the door with a lot more force than was needed. Before she walked through the rain to the house, she turned back to the car. "By the way, I quit." Then she hurried away. Behind her, she heard Cole back out of the driveway and go down the road toward town.

Not until she got on the porch did she realize the door was

ajar. *Darn!* She must have been in such a hurry this morning that she never pulled it all the way closed. But what if someone was in there? She reached for her cell phone to call Cole, and then stopped. If the house was empty and she was just being paranoid, she'd look like a fool in front of him, and she'd already done that once today.

Nevertheless, just to be on the safe side, she pushed it open and peered in before she went inside. Her heart beat so loud in her ears she was sure if anyone lay in wait they'd hear it. Beads of sweat joined the raindrops running down her forehead. She clutched her purse by the handles as if it were a club. It wouldn't do much damage, but it might give her time to get away from any would-be assailant.

As she scanned the living room, she listened for the sound of an intruder. When she heard nothing, she slipped quietly inside, making certain to leave the front door wide open, just in case. Her back stiff, her senses on high alert, she carefully checked each room one by one. As room after room turned up empty and undisturbed, her heartbeat slowly resumed its normal rate. When the last one also proved to be without an unwanted occupant, she breathed a deep sigh of relief. Her whole body and her death grip on her purse handles relaxed.

As she made her way back through the living room and closed the front door, she felt a bit foolish. Who would want to break into her house? There certainly wasn't anything here of value, and any burglar would leave sorely disappointed.

She'd obviously jumped to the wrong conclusion and the door had been ajar simply because she hadn't pulled it close when she'd left. Nothing more.

Because of her apprehension about the open door, her anger at Cole had cooled and now lay in a big ball of disillusionment in her stomach. She'd thought him beyond lies and deceit, but once more her judgment of men proved to be less than accurate. When would she learn?

She'd trusted Cole. Hadn't she? No. She hadn't. Not really. Despite everything he'd done for her and Lizzie, one indisputable truth remained. Cole Ainsley was a man. And her track record in that department left little room for trust in him, or any man.

FAITH HAD JUST put a pot of water on to boil in preparation for making Lizzie's favorite, mac and cheese, when a knock sounded on the door. She turned down the flame under the pot, wiped her hands on a paper towel, and then went to the door. Holding her breath and praying it wasn't Cole, she swung the door open.

"Momma!" Lizzie launched herself from Granny Jo's arms into Faith's.

Faith kissed Lizzie's sweet cheek. "Hello, my sweet baby girl. Did you have a good time with Granny?"

"Oh, yes." Granny stepped inside as Faith held the door wider for her. "We had a very good time. Didn't we, Lizzie?" She chucked the child under the chin. Lizzie clutched her teddy bear closer, curled her chin into her neck, and giggled. "Lizzie and my old hound, Jake, became fast friends. He never left her side. You might think about getting her a dog. She sure loves them. Make a good playmate for her."

"I'll think about it. We'll be having supper soon." Faith motioned for Granny to take a seat on the sofa. She sat next her with Lizzie on her lap. "I'd be pleased if you'd join us. Nothing fancy, just Lizzie's favorite mac and cheese."

"Thank you for the invite, but Becky has asked me to come for supper. But I'll take a rain check."

Faith smiled. "Anytime. You're always welcome." Just having Granny sitting in her living room eased the stiffness from Faith's tangled nerves. She reminded her of her grandmother, the one person in her life who had made Faith feel worthwhile and loved. She shifted a squirming Lizzie to the floor. "So how was your day with my little hellion?"

Granny didn't answer. Instead, she studied Faith with those wise, knowing eyes of hers. "Suppose you tell me how your first day at your job went."

Granny's word brought back all the animosity she'd felt

about Cole's deceit. A tight fist formed in Faith's chest. She really didn't want to talk about her day, but Granny's gentle hand on hers coaxed the words from her. "I quit."

Granny sat up straight. "Well, that's a bit of a surprise. May I ask why?"

For a long moment, Faith refrained from explaining. How could she admit she'd been taken in again by a man, even to this compassionate woman? Some of the anger she'd felt when she'd discovered Cole's lie rose up in her throat like sour bile. She swallowed it down. "He lied to me, Granny Jo." She told Granny everything from the time she'd walked into Cole's house until she'd slammed out of his car.

"Darlin'," Granny said softly, "men lie. It's in their DNA. Poor dears can't help it. Lord knows my Earl told his share of them. They think if they concoct some outlandish tale that it's better than the truth, and it'll get them out of trouble." She laughed. "Most times, it just digs their hole deeper. From what you've told me, it appears that Cole might have been lying for a good reason." She patted Faith's hand. "My advice is, you should let him explain. You might be surprised at what he tells you."

Granny stood, and, after kissing Lizzie goodbye, walked toward the door. With her hand on the knob, she paused and turned back to Faith. "From all I've heard, Cole is a good man. You may want to keep that in mind. Just because the good didn't take in some men, God didn't shut down the factory."

Faith stared at the closed door for several minutes after Granny Jo left. Could she be right? Had Faith misjudged Cole's motives?

Lizzie let out a wail. Faith roused herself from her thoughts. Poor Lizzie. Faith had gotten so engrossed in her own troubles that she forgot the poor baby was probably hungry. "Momma's making supper, sweet thing." She hurried off to the kitchen to add the pasta to the rapidly boiling water. Then she went back in the living room and picked up her daughter. "Momma's sorry. Supper will be ready in just a bit."

The sound of a car in the driveway drew her attention from

Lizzie. Cole? Apprehension riding heavy on her shoulders, she carried Lizzie to the living room and peeked around the curtain. What she saw took her breath away.

Just what she needed to cap off an already crappy day.

Chapter 9

FAITH GRITTED HER teeth and opened her front door for her impromptu visitor. She stared into a face that she knew so well and had hoped she'd not have to see until she steeled herself for the meeting.

"Hello, Mother."

"Faith." Celia Chambers looked from Faith to Lizzie. The uncompromising line of the woman's mouth clearly exhibited her condemnation of the child.

Lizzie seemed to sense her grandmother's censure and cuddled closer to Faith. Fuzzy was clutched so tightly against the child that his head was bent backwards.

Celia turned her attention away from the cowering child and back to Faith. When she spoke, her tone was cold and un-relenting. "Since you seem to have forgotten your manners and never came to call on your daddy and me, I decided that I'd come to you. However, you could have come to your home and said hello."

Disbelief washed over Faith. Not for a moment did she think that her mother missed her, or her reason for showing up here unannounced was as simple as a social call on her "wayward daughter." Faith almost said that she'd planned to stop by, but it was a lie, and her mother was an expert at telling when her only daughter was lying.

Instead, Faith said, "*This* is my home, Mother."

Her mother looked around the small, but neat living room. She raised one eyebrow. "Hmm, such as it is." She turned back to Faith. "Are you going to ask me in, or have you forgotten everything I taught you?"

Forgotten? Not likely. Faith remembered every excruciating moment of her childhood. It still had the power to make her want to scream that God never intended for people to be like her mother. He wanted children to be happy and to live lives that didn't include being reprimanded for breathing the wrong way "because they'd go to hell." And her father should have stood up for his daughter, not hovered silently in the shadows while she endured her mother's unrelenting rules and reprimands.

Faith stepped aside and prayed that this visit would be brief. "Come in, Mother. Have a seat."

Celia walked to the sofa, looked at it for a moment, and then sat on the very edge, as if getting ready to run if some warrior germ should launch an attack on her. Faith had forgotten her mother's aversion to dirt, among a long list of other things that had caused her to turn up her nose. Dirt and germs wouldn't have dared cross the threshold of the Chambers' home. Faith refused to make Lizzie grow up in the same antiseptic surroundings that she had. She wanted the house to be clean but comfortable.

While her mother arranged the dark brown skirt of her dress just so, Faith took stock of the woman who had raised her. Celia rarely smiled, so no laugh lines creased the skin around her mouth. Contrarily, the frown lines across her forehead had dug deep furrows in the skin. Blue eyes, the color of a frozen lake, held no emotion. More gray peppered her dark brown hair than Faith recalled being there before. All in all, if Celia had ever been attractive, her unbending outlook on people and life in general had stolen her looks long ago.

Faith took a seat across from her mother in a large, comfy armchair that had seen better days. "Why are you here, Mother? Just to tell me what a bad housekeeper I am and what a sinful life I've led?"

"There's no need to get snippy with me, young lady." Her mother frowned. "Do I need a reason to visit my only daughter and . . . her daughter?"

The woman couldn't even acknowledge her own granddaughter. Frothing anger bubble up inside Faith. Her mother could think as little of Faith as she wanted, but she was *not* going to label Lizzie. She glared at the woman who had given birth to her. "Lizzie is your granddaughter. Is that so hard for you to say?"

"Yes, it is. I can't turn a blind eye to sin." Her mother huffed and folded her hands primly in her lap. "You have no one to blame but yourself for how I feel, Faith, and how miserably your life has turned out. You chose to move to that godless city and live in sin. And if that wasn't bad enough, you compounded your sin by giving birth to a child out of wedlock."

Enough! Faith suddenly felt like the teenager who had done something un-Christian in the eyes of her judgmental mother and was about to be reprimanded for it. Incredibly, Celia had momentarily transformed Faith back to the young girl who'd cringed under her mother's sharp tongue. In the old days, she would have taken the tongue lashing and skulked off to her room.

Not anymore.

Faith vaulted to her feet. "What do you want, Mother?" She was certain that her mother had not suddenly showed up on her daughter's doorstep for a coffee klatch.

Celia stood and faced Faith with an icy stare. "Well, if you're going to be like that, I might as well say it. I want my mother's locket."

The request shocked Faith. Her grandmother had not gotten along with her daughter. However, Faith and Gramma Harrison had been very close. She'd been on her deathbed when she'd given Faith the locket. Celia had never shown any interest in the piece of jewelry before. The plain gold locket had a rose and an imitation ruby on the front. Hardly an expensive piece of jewelry. Celia had never been interested in it before. Why now?

"Grandma Harrison gave that to me on her deathbed."

Celia's expression took on an almost evil look. "Your grandmother and I never saw eye-to-eye, but whatever else she was, she was a God-fearing woman. If she had known how you would turn out, despite my efforts to prevent it, she would not want a . . . a—"

"Go ahead. Say it, Mother. A harlot. A sinner."

Celia started, obviously surprised that her venom had been

met with venom. But she didn't back down. "Yes. A sinner. That's what you became the day you moved in with that man and slept with him without the bonds of matrimony."

Lizzie's lower lip protruded, a sure sign that the raised voices were scaring her, and she would burst into tears at any moment.

Faith cuddled her daughter closer and lowered her voice. "Well, you're not getting it. It's mine."

Celia Chambers stalked to the door and yanked it open. Then she turned back to her daughter, hot anger shooting from her eyes. "I will get it. Count on it." She slammed the door behind her hard enough to make the glass in the windows rattle.

WITH SUPPER DONE and Lizzie bedded down for the night, Faith collapsed on the sofa and breathed a deep sigh. What a day it had been. She fingered the gold locket hanging from the chain around her neck.

Though a bit on the eccentric side, Gramma Harrison had been the light of Faith's young life, the one loving presence throughout most of her early childhood. Memories assailed her, and a chuckle escaped Faith. After a bank foreclosed on her and Grampa's house, Gramma had not trusted banks. She swore she'd never entrust a cent to one again. As a solution, when their lumber business became one of the biggest in the county, she'd taken to hiding money all over her house: in couch pillows, in the freezer of her fridge, in the cellar in her canning jars, and any other number of places. Each hiding place contained anywhere from a handful of coins to several hundred dollars. When Faith's parents had cleaned out the old woman's house, they'd found enough money to buy her mother a good used car. Celia had always been sure they'd missed some of the hidden cash.

Because Faith was so young, the money had never interested her. When Gramma Harrison died, nine-year-old Faith was inconsolable, unable to understand why this God that her mother had said loved her would take the most important person in her life away from her. She'd drowned her sorrows in the fur of the teddy bear, a gift from her grandmother, that years later Lizzie would call Fuzzy and adopt as her constant companion. Faith had kept it, determined to give it to her child, and it delighted her that Lizzie loved the stuffed toy as much as her mother had.

As if it were yesterday, Faith remembered what her grandmother's constant promise to her. "I will always take care of you, sweet girl, even from heaven."

She looked at the ceiling. "I could sure use some of that help right now, Gramma."

Faith's visit to the past was suddenly interrupted by her cell phone's strident ringing. Quickly, she grabbed it off the coffee table. Only Cole and Granny Jo had her number. She glanced at the caller ID. Cole.

Faith searched for the anger she'd felt for him not long ago, but it had drained away. Replacing it was an unreasonable need to see him again. She needed his strength and caring hand holding hers. She rested the phone against her ear. "Hello."

"Hi." Cole's deep voice rumbled through the phone and tripped over every one of her nerve endings. "I'm almost to your house. If I pull into your driveway, are you gonna shoot at me?" Cautious humor colored his outrageous question.

Suddenly, her troubles of the day melted away. Why was it that just the sound of his voice erased all the stress from her life? She laughed. "Yep. But because I kind of like you, you get a choice between my Super Soaker or my paintball gun."

He laughed. "I'll leave that up to you. Whichever one you think I deserve for my stupidity."

Faith hung up as a car pulled into her driveway. Feeling anxious, she went to the door and swung it open. The rain had stopped and the sun was out. Cole was just getting out of his squad car and walking toward her. Her breath caught as she watched him approach looking like a muscular panther stalking his prey. Undeniable strength transmitted itself in the way his broad shoulders strained against the black material of his uniform shirt. His powerful thighs filled out the legs of his gray pants. Since he'd left his hat in the squad car, the sun glinted off his dark black hair, leaving bluish highlights to shine through. She couldn't deny that he was one of the handsomest men she'd ever seen.

While fighting the smile that wanted to curve her mouth, she gave him a curt nod and stepped aside for him to enter the house. "Good evening, Sheriff."

Cole grinned at her and inclined his head. "Evenin', ma'am."

That she wasn't still mad at him, or at least didn't appear to be, surprised him. When she'd slammed the car door that afternoon and stomped off into her house, he was sure she had enough mad in her to last for a good long time. "I'm assuming I'm forgiven." She opened her mouth to reply, but he held up his hand. "I still owe you an explanation."

"Since we're about to have a serious talk, I'd rather do it over coffee." She walked ahead of him into the kitchen.

He looked around. "Where's Lizzie?" He hadn't seen the toddler in a while and was hoping she'd be around now.

"Hopefully asleep." Faith filled the glass carafe with water and then poured it into the well of the coffeemaker.

The aroma of ground coffee drifted to Cole. Oddly, it made him feel like he'd come home after a long day. For a long time, he just watched Faith as she finished preparing the coffee, the sway of her hips, her lithe, almost fragile body, the way her blond hair caressed her shoulders. Then he remembered something she'd said on the phone. "So you *kind of* like me, huh?"

She glanced over her shoulder and grinned. "Kind of."

Lord help him, there were so many things about Faith he was discovering, things that could really grow on him . . . and were. She had a dynamite body, a quick sense of humor and an easy smile. Didn't hold onto a grudge the way Diane had. Loved her beautiful little daughter above all else. As an added bonus, he'd watched her with Lizzie and come to the conclusion that she had an inner beauty that matched her physical beauty.

When the coffee was done, she poured two cups and placed them on the table. And she was as much of a coffee addict as he was. Big plus. But if he had any hope of their friendship blossoming into anything more, he had some explaining to do.

He waited while she added milk and sugar to her coffee.

He folded his hands around the hot cup, taking a strange comfort in the heat that permeated his palms.

"You were going to explain." She raised an eyebrow. "Let's hear it."

Chapter 10

COLE LOOKED ACROSS Faith's kitchen table and searched for the words to explain to her why a supposedly mature man would trash his own house, and then hire her to clean it up. In retrospect, it had to have been the craziest thing he'd ever done, and anything he offered as a reason at this point would only confirm that. But he had to try.

"First of all," he finally said and looked her directly in the eyes, "I'm so sorry about that whole thing at my house. I never meant to hurt you or upset you."

"Then why? Why did you do it?"

He looked down into the dark liquid in his cup and ran a fingertip around the rim. "Honestly, I worried about you and Lizzie not having any means of support." Then, recalling that he'd always spotted a liar in an interview when they wouldn't make eye contact, he raised his gaze to meet hers. "I figured out from your reaction to our grocery shopping trip that you aren't really keen on taking help from others. So I thought that by giving you a job I could help, and you wouldn't feel like it was charity. But when I looked around my house, I realized that it was too clean. So I messed it up." He'd been right. It did sound crazy.

Faith's eyes filled with tears. One ran down her cheek. *Good going, Ainsley. Now you've made her cry.* "Oh, darn it! Faith, I—"

She raised a hand and stopped him. "Wait. Let me talk now."

For a moment, emotion overwhelmed Faith and stole her voice. His explanation had been so simple, yet so sincere. Any remaining remnants of the anger she'd felt for Cole's deception vanished. Faith gulped down the emotions clogging her throat.

"In all the time I knew Sloan, I could never imagine him doing anything like this for me. Half the time, he didn't remember to give me money to shop for food." She swallowed back more tears. "You were right about my feelings toward taking charity. When I came back to Carson, I swore that I would not rely on anyone ever again. I didn't want their offerings of pity. I was determined to take care of us without anyone's help. But just as I did when I went to Atlanta, I came home without any plan." She smiled weakly. "That seems to be my MO."

Cole grabbed both her hands in his. The strength of his grip and the warmth on his skin on hers, stirred feelings in Faith that she'd thought died long ago. "Sweetheart, there's no shame in taking help when it's offered, especially when you have a little one to consider. People aren't doing it out of pity. They're doing it out of love."

Sweetheart? Love? What was he trying to say?

Just as quickly, she chastised herself for attempting to read more into his words than were really there. *Don't start building tomorrows that will never come,* she told herself.

"In my heart, I know that. I guess that's the only reason I've accepted what I have so far. But when I realized what you'd done, that you'd lied to me, I just got so . . . so . . ."

"I know, and I am as sorry as I can be that I made you feel that way. It was not intentional. If I'd thought it through more, I would have seen that." He tucked his finger under her chin, tipped it up so she had to look at him, and smiled. "Forgiven?"

She nodded. "Forgiven. But promise me that you won't lie to me again."

"Promise."

Not until that moment did Faith realized Cole still had a grip on her hands. She eased them from his grasp, rose and retrieved the coffee pot, and busied herself with refreshing their coffee, coffee that neither of them had touched.

"Explaining my stupidity wasn't the only reason I came here." Cole leaned back in his chair. "I have some good news for you." He sipped his coffee.

A quick flash of her confrontation with her mother passed through her mind. "I could use some good news." She sighed.

"After you dropped me off, I found my front door open. Then my mother—"

Cole straightened and leaned toward her. "Wait! Your front door was open?" Concern filled his expression. Faith could almost see his law enforcement training materialize.

"It was nothing. I checked the house, and there wasn't anyone here."

Cole frowned and leaned forward, his elbows on the table. "Please tell me you didn't do that."

Her cheeks burned with embarrassment at having to admit her foolhardiness. "Yeah, I did. But as I said, no one was here. Nothing was disturbed." She shrugged. "I must have been in such a hurry when you picked me up that I didn't latch it all the way." That she'd been so careless in so many ways made her feel foolish all over again.

Cole didn't seem satisfied with her explanation. "You have to be more careful. Promise you won't do that again. Call me first."

"I promise." Eager to shift the conversation away from this subject, she asked, "So, what's the good news you have for me?"

"Hunter Mackenzie, the local vet, needs a receptionist."

Was this another of his invented jobs?

He must have read the skepticism in her expression. "Before you jump to any conclusions, I didn't make this one up or harass Hunter into hiring you. Doc Amos called me today. It seems Hunter's wife, Rose, is having some problems with her pregnancy, and Doc wants her to keep off her feet and cut down on any stress for the remaining few months. The job's not permanent, but at least it'll give you an income for a few months while you look for something else. It's yours if you want it."

Finally! A job!

She and Lizzie would make it. Nerves that had been stretched to the breaking point relaxed. The constant fear she'd carried with her since coming back to Carson was replaced by a growing excitement. Suddenly, the elation ebbed just as fast as it had materialized. "But I don't know anything about being a receptionist."

Cole laughed. The sound washed over Faith like a warm summer breeze. "You can answer a phone, right?" Faith nodded. "You can make appointments, right?" Again, she nodded. "Well, that's all you need to know. Hunter has a nurse to help in the clinic, so you just need to man the phone and write in his appointment book." He finished his coffee and stood. "I'll pick you up tomorrow morning and take you out there."

"Wait." Something that could blow this opportunity came to Faith. "You can take me tomorrow, but what about after that? How am I going to get to work every day?"

Cole grinned. "Got that covered, too. For the time being, I'll take you. In the meantime, young lady, I'm going to teach you to drive so you can get your license and use my car."

Learning wasn't a problem. She'd taken a full year of Drivers' Ed in high school, passed it with flying colors, and still recalled most of what she'd learned. However, using his car? "But—"

He laid a finger over her lips. "No *buts* about it." When she continued to try to protest, he continued. "Please let me do this to make up for the housekeeper thing. It's no problem. I don't need my other car. If I do need transportation, I have the squad car at my disposal all the time, and it will help you achieve that independence you want so badly." He started toward the door with Faith following close behind.

"Cole?" He stopped and turned back to her. She hoisted herself on tiptoe and kissed his cheek. "Thank you," she whispered against his skin. And she meant it. He'd done more for her in the short time she'd known him than Sloan had done in the entire time they'd been together.

He turned his head just a fraction and looked down at her. Faith's breath caught. His whiskey eyes captured hers. Mesmerized by the desire burning in their depths, she was unable to move, unable to turn away from the inevitable, unable to stop what her head told her was not a good idea, but her heart brushed aside.

Very slowly, as if giving her time to refuse, he lowered his head. Refusal never entered Faith's mind. Need overrode her good sense. Instead of stopping Cole, she found herself leaning against his muscular body and sliding her hands up his broad chest. Shamelessly, she tipped her head back and offered him her lips. When his mouth settled gently over hers, her knees turned to rubber, and had it not been for his arms encircling her waist, she would have sunk to the floor in a boneless heap.

The kiss that started out sweet, soft, and gentle, quickly turned hungry and passionate. Faith clung to him, her arms wrapped around his neck, pulling him closer. Desire eroded her willpower like ocean waves eating away at a sandy beach. He lifted his head, breathed her name, and then captured her mouth again. This time, she felt as if he was branding her forever with his kiss.

"Momma!"

Lizzie's strident cry pulled them apart as if they'd been drenched in icy water. She stared up at him, at a loss for words. He touched her face reverently. "I'd best go before we do something we'll both be sorry for tomorrow." He ran his fingertips over her cheek as if memorizing the shape and texture, then released her, and opened the door. "I'll be by around eight for you."

Faith didn't trust her voice. She nodded and after the door closed behind him, she sagged against it and stood there for a moment, unable to get her feet to move.

"Momma!"

Shaking herself out of the sensual stupor she'd been trapped in, Faith hurried off toward Lizzie's room. "Momma's coming, baby."

COLE POURED HIS morning coffee and carried it to the front porch. He flopped down in one of the rockers he'd bought yesterday, because Faith had been right about the rockers. He took a sip of the coffee and waited for the jolt of caffeine to hit his system and bring his sleep-deprived body to life.

It wasn't often that he got up early enough to enjoy the dawn, but last night and into this morning, sleep had stubbornly eluded him. The idea of sitting out here and watching the sun rise above Hawks Mountain appealed to his need for serenity. Intentionally, he cleared his mind and concentrated on the changing hues of orange, purple, and pink as the sun gradually peeked over the mountain. Except for the few white puffs hanging over the peeks of Hawks Mountain, the sky was clear. It was going to be a beautiful day. Heaving a deep sigh of contentment, he started the rocking chair moving in a gentle back and forth motion.

Just beyond the porch, a squirrel scampered over the sun-dappled grass. A soft *whit-chew whit-chew* drew his gaze to the birdfeeder hanging from a huge oak tree just beyond the porch railing. A female cardinal scooped up the sunflower seeds, her drab, brown body almost obscured by the backdrop of the tree's bark. In the maple tree on the other side of the lawn, a flash of brilliant red told Cole that her male counterpart was standing guard over his mate. When the squirrel headed toward the feeder, the male swooped down, putting himself between the squirrel and the female cardinal. Alerted to the intrusion by the raucous cry of the male, the female flew off, followed almost immediately by the male.

The whole scenario served to bring his thoughts back to Faith. If only she'd accept his help and protection as readily as the female cardinal accepted her mate's. But Faith was fiercely independent—a trait he admired, even if it did frustrate him. In a way, it was good that she didn't want to rely on him. What would happen to her when he left for Atlanta and his new job? He didn't want to be the cause of her feeling as helpless as she had when she'd arrived back in Carson.

So what brilliant move had he made last night? He'd kissed her. And not just a friendly peck on the lips. He'd kissed her as if his very life depended on feeling her lips beneath his, and, at that moment, it had. Under different circumstances, her response would have filled him with joy, and it had . . . last night.

But now that he'd had time to reflect on it, he realized it had been a huge mistake. It would have been different if he planned on putting down roots in Carson and settling in to raise a family here. But he wasn't, and if he continued encouraging Faith to believe otherwise, it could bring both of them nothing but heartache when he left town. That could not happen.

Having made up his mind to call a halt to any further intimacy with Faith, he felt a bit better. He leaned back in the rocker and set it into motion again. Faith would love the rockers and so would Lizzie. And that thought resurrected the memory of Lizzie's strident cry for her mother which brought with it the memory of the kiss.

Try as he might, and no matter how many times he resolved not to think about her, she kept invading his thoughts. The feel of her lips beneath his, the way she'd clung to him, the contours of her body fitting so perfectly with his. All of it persistently played through his mind like a favorite movie stuck in rerun mode.

Heaving a deep sigh, he stopped the rocker's motion and leaned forward, resting his forearms on his thighs and gazed down into his cooling coffee. *The heart has a mind of its own.* His mother's words to him after the breakup with Diane played through his head. At the time, he'd shrugged them off, but now he hoped her well-worn quote was wrong. If it wasn't, he was going to end up hurting the person he wanted to protect, the one person who didn't deserve any more hurt in her life.

Chapter 11

FAITH SAT BESIDE Cole in the reception area of the Paws and Claws Animal Clinic and Wildlife Sanctuary and waited for Dr. Hunter Mackenzie to pronounce his final verdict on whether or not Faith had a job.

Dr. Mackenzie was seated behind the receptionist desk reading the pitiful resume Faith had managed to scrape together and handwrote last night. As he read, she studied him. Granny Jo had told her that he'd met his wife Rose when she applied for a job as his receptionist. She had been a surrogate mother for her close friend, and the friend and her husband had died in a car accident, leaving Rose to carry the twins she'd conceived and to take care of them after they were born. Rose and Hunter had fallen in love and married, and he adored his adopted twin daughters.

Maybe Granny was right. Maybe there were a few good men. Faith glanced at the man beside her and then shifted in the uncomfortable, molded plastic chair.

"You okay?" Cole kept his voice low.

Cole had stayed until they knew what Hunter would say so she'd have a ride home. At first, she had wanted him to leave and let her call him when the verdict was in, but now she was glad he'd insisted on waiting with her. Just his presence beside her gave her the courage to face Hunter's final decision, no matter what it would be. She wanted to grab Cole's hand and siphon off the strength she knew she'd find there, but she didn't. Instead, she clutched her hands together in her lap until her fingers ached.

Faith offered him a weak smile. "I'm fine. Just a bit anxious."

Just before the feeling left her fingers, Cole pried her hands apart, enclosed one in his, and smiled down at her. "Relax. I'm sure you've got this in the bag."

His reassurance helped calm some of the anxiety she'd been feeling since she'd gotten out of bed that morning. She didn't understand why she was feeling so uptight. After all, she'd had job interviews up and down Carson's Main Street and managed it without balancing on the edge of a nervous overload.

But none of them had been your last option. This one is, a little voice inside her head taunted. *What will you do if you don't get this job? Go back to "cleaning" Cole's clean house?*

She shivered as a chill of apprehension danced up her spine. "What if—"

Cole squeezed her hand gently. "Think positive. I am. He'd be crazy not to hire you."

A smile teased at the corners of her mouth. "You're prejudiced."

"Yup." He winked, and her heart nearly burst from her chest.

What was there about this man that had the power to make her believe that the sun would always shine on her days, and that there really was a tomorrow waiting just around the next corner?

Whoa, girl! Dangerous thinking. Just like that kiss was last night.

Cole was no different than any other man she'd ever come in contact with in her life. Her father had stood stoically aside while her mother pounded her Bible and berated Faith and declared she'd go to hell for her transgressions. Sloan had taken all she had to give and given nothing but heartache in return. Cole had lied to get his way, something she'd forgiven him for, but couldn't forget. All in all, her scorecard with men registered a big, bold, fat zero.

"Faith." Dr. Mackenzie's voice pulled her from her thoughts.

She would have stood, but her legs were just too shaky. Finally, she forced herself to her feet and approached the desk. "Yes?"

He waved the resume in the air. "Not much here."

Heat suffused her face. She lowered her gaze to her hand still holding Cole's. "No, sir."

Dr. Mackenzie smiled. "When I hired my wife, she knew

nothing about this business, but she became one of my greatest assets. I have a young boy who works with me and has no training, but he's better with my animals than I am." He waved the paper again. "Words on paper don't always tell me the best things about a person. I've learned to rely on my instincts. And my instincts tell me you're a good person." The handsome vet smiled at her. "The job's yours if you want it. You can start tomorrow, but please call me Hunter. Sir is way too formal for a place where cleaning up animal poop is a regular part of a day's work."

IN THE CAR, FAITH leaned back against the seat, a huge smile across her lips. "I can't believe it. I'm gainfully employed," she announced because she had to hear the words to make sure it was true.

"That you are." Cole started the squad car and steered it out of the parking lot. "And I think we need to celebrate. Can Granny Jo keep Lizzie a few hours longer?"

"Probably. Why?"

He grinned at her, and then quickly shifted his gaze back to the winding road leading from the vet's office to the main highway. "Because I'm taking you to dinner at the Lodge at the Lake."

In her heart, Faith knew this would probably be playing Russian roulette with fate, but the idea of going out to dinner and spending the evening with Cole was too tempting. "I'll call Granny."

Granny Jo not only agreed to keep Lizzie longer, she'd insisted on keeping her overnight and ordered Faith to relax and enjoy celebrating getting a job.

TIKI TORCHES stationed strategically along the railing illuminated the darkness. Candles in glass globes placed on each of the tables cast a golden glow over the Lodge at the Lake's patio diners. Cole leaned back, comfortably sated by his lobster dinner. When she'd told him she'd never had lobster before and seemed reluctant to choose from the expensive items on the menu, with her permission, he'd ordered lobster, loaded baked potato, and a salad for her.

Faith laid down her fork and placed her open palm against her stomach and groaned. "I think if I put one more forkful of food in my mouth, I'll burst."

He frowned. "That's too bad. I'm told the chef here is famous for his desserts, but I guess you won't have room for the *crème brûlée* then."

Faith's mouth curled up in an enticing smile. "I have no idea what that is, but just the name sounds heavenly. Want to share one with me?"

Dessert wasn't the only thing he wanted to share with her, but he pushed that thought aside, nodded, and motioned for the waiter. The young man sidled up to their table, and Cole ordered one dessert and two coffees. When the order came, there was only one dessert spoon. Cole picked it up, broke through the caramelized crust, and then scooped out some of the creamy custard beneath it. He held out the spoon to her. "Try it."

As her lips closed around it, a hot stab of awareness zipped through Cole's lower body. He tried to avert his gaze, but he might as well have been trying to drain the lake with a sip straw. As though that hadn't been enough of a strain on his libido, once she got the custard off the spoon and into her mouth, she licked her lips and sighed. He stifled a groan and averted his gaze to the moon-washed lake. But, as if magnetized, his attention went back to her.

"You have to try some." Faith extended the spoon to him. "I was right. It's heavenly."

Cole shook his head. "I just can't fit any more food in me." He indicated that she retain the spoon. "You finish it." Then he tortured himself by watching her eat the rest of the creamy dessert.

Despite being outside in the cool mountain air, by the time they'd finished dinner and paid the guest check, Cole was certain the temperature on the patio had risen to near the boiling point.

"Could we take a walk by the lake?" Faith asked.

Cole was stunned into silence. He'd been certain she'd want to go home right after dinner. Evidently, his hesitation made her think he didn't want to do it.

"It's okay if you don't want to. You must be tired, and you've already done so much for me today. If you'd rather go home . . ."

Even though he knew it probably wasn't the brightest move he'd ever made, he was not about to end this evening any faster than he had to. He immediately accepted her suggestion. "Walk by the lake it is." He took her arm and steered her toward the staircase that led from the upper patio to the lakeside below.

As they reached the bottom of the stairs, his hand slipped down her arm to encase her hand in his. For a long time, they strolled silently, hand-in-hand, soaking up the sights and sounds of the night.

The wind blew across the surface of the lake and produced tiny waves that rushed the shore and lapped gently at the bank. The moving water caught the reflection of the full moon and caused splashes of silvery light to dance over the surface of the lake. A dog barked in the distance. Night creatures skittered through the underbrush, disturbed by the intrusion of the humans in their midst.

Faith's contented sigh broke the silence. "I feel as if the weight of the world has been lifted off my shoulders. Having a job and an income, even if it'll only be until Rose comes back to work, is such a relief. I can even plan a small birthday party for Lizzie."

"It's Lizzie's birthday?"

A balmy breeze blew in off the lake, ruffling Faith's hair across her cheeks. Before she could push it away, Cole's fingers brushed her face, captured the flyaway strands, and anchored them behind her ear. His touch ignited a flame deep inside her that warmed her through and through.

"Her birthday is in a few weeks. She'll be three. I was afraid I'd have to make believe it was just another day. But not now." She grinned, trying not to acknowledge what his touch was doing to her insides, but pleased that she would be able to give

Lizzie something she'd never had before. "Not that she'd know, of course." She moved away, out of his reach.

For a moment he stared at her, then asked, "Am I invited?"

Faith laughed in an effort to make light of the moment. "She'd never forgive me if I didn't invite her favorite fella."

"I'll come, but you have to let me get the cake. My sister has a little business making cakes for special occasions, and this is definitely special. After all, how often does a gal turn three?"

Cole took Faith's hand and guided her over a fallen log. As she stepped over it, her foot caught on a broken twig protruding from the limb. She stumbled and would have fallen if Cole hadn't caught her in his arms. Instantly, her laughter died. She stared up at him, acutely aware of the thump of his heart against her chest.

"Cole." His whispered name hung on the lake breeze.

Lord help him, Cole knew what he was about to do was exactly what he'd promised himself he wouldn't do again, but her lips were just too close, too tempting, too inviting. He leaned down, slowly closing the space between them. Her warm breath feathered his face just before his lips touched hers.

The kiss they'd shared the other night had been passionate, but brief because of Lizzie's interruption, but tonight there was no interruption, and it seemed to go on forever. Cole kept telling himself to stop, but everything inside him defied the command. Instead, he folded Faith closer in his arms and intensified the kiss.

Faith moaned deep in her throat and tightened her arms around his neck, pulling his lips down hard on hers. Heat shot through Cole like a flaming arrow. Caution raised its ugly head. This was going too fast. Against his will, he lifted his head and gazed down at her desire-soaked eyes.

"I think we'd better get out of here." He didn't recognize the raspy voice that had said those words.

Faith slammed back to earth with a resounding *thump*. Instantly, she released him and stumbled backward as though she'd been burned. Cole caught her again, but this time kept her at arm's length. She lowered her gaze. "Yes, I guess we'd better."

Slowly, and this time without touching, they made their way silently back the way they'd come. Faith's entire body burned with need and gave no sign of cooling. Her lips still throbbed from the kiss, but she couldn't believe how she'd responded to Cole. If he hadn't stopped the kiss, she knew she wouldn't have been able to. God help her, she'd wanted it to go on forever. Truth be known, and as dangerous as it could be to her heart, she wanted him to kiss her again and again until she forgot everything but Cole Ainsley.

COLE PULLED THE car into her driveway and turned off the ignition. He held out his hand. "Give me your house keys. I'm going in first to make sure everything is all right." Recalling what had happened the last time she came home, Faith laid them in his palm without question. "Stay here until I call you." Cole left the car and hurried to the front door. Seconds later, he disappeared inside the house.

Several long minutes passed before a light came on in the living room window. While Faith waited, she relived their kiss over and over. Her body thrummed with the need to go further. Cole reappeared on her porch and motioned for her to get out of the car. She climbed out and made her way to the front porch where he waited for her.

"Everything is okay," he said, handing her keys back to her. "Lock the door after I leave."

She tucked the keys in her pocket and nodded. "I will. And . . . thanks for everything, Cole."

"Everything?"

She couldn't see his face, but she could hear the intimation in his voice. Was he referring to the kiss they'd shared by the lake?

He shifted slightly, and the light from the window illuminated his face. His dark gaze bore into her, sending shivers of desire coursing over her, reigniting the flames that had consumed her at the lake. His look silently said the same thing she'd been saying to herself since they'd pulled part on the lake shore.

I want you.

The fire she could feel eating at her inside burst into a consuming flame, turning her resistance to ashes. At that moment, she made a decision she knew she might come to regret later, but right now . . .

Without saying a word, she took his hand and led him inside the house and closed the door.

Chapter 12

COLE GLANCED AT the clock. He'd been sitting in his darkened living room for over two hours, ever since he'd slipped out of Faith's house as she slept, and made his way home. However, sleep had eluded him. He sipped at the can of beer that had grown warm in his hand. His thoughts ricocheted between knowing that making love to Faith tonight had opened a door he had not wanted opened and wanting to go back there and crawl back into bed with her.

The latter choice, as much as he wanted it, was not going to happen. It would only add another brick to the wall that would eventually collapse on both of them. He didn't need any more heartache, and Faith had already had enough pain to last a lifetime.

Taking the last sip of the beer, he crushed the can in his fist. Then he threw it on the coffee table, barely mindful of how it skidded across the table and dropped to the floor. His concentration remained centered on his problem.

Having painted himself into a corner by promising not only to drive her to work but to also give her driving lessons after work, Cole had laid temptation right in his path. He couldn't back out. Faith was depending on him. So what was the answer?

He strode to the window and stared out at his front lawn where the moonlight painted eerie shadows across the grass. Behind him, the clock ticked away the minutes until he would have to come face to face with her again.

Protecting her from the pitfalls of life had always been number one on his list. Now it seemed that the one thing that posed the most dangerous threat to her was Cole Ainsley. Being with her on a daily basis had already intensified his initial attraction, luring him into something that he wasn't able to control.

The only answer was to call on the willpower he'd used as a detective on the streets of Richmond. He'd have to put up a barricade between Faith Chambers and his emotions.

FAITH WOKE UP and rolled to her side. Stretching out her hand, she felt the cold, empty bed beside her. She slid her hand to the pillow and traced the dent left by Cole's head. Then, while memories of their love making danced through her head, she buried her face in the pillow and inhaled his fragrance.

She'd only been with two other men in her life: Ronnie Connors, who had taken her virginity in her senior year and left her wondering what all the fuss was about, and Sloan, who had been more concerned with his own satisfaction than hers. So her basis for comparison was somewhat limited, but Cole had been far and above anything she'd experienced before. He'd been a gentle, caring lover who had held her afterward and whispered sweet things in her ear until she fell asleep in his arms.

Without warning, doubts and regret stole the beautiful memories of the night before. Not until now did she realize that she had expected Cole to be there when morning came. Why had he slipped away while she slept? Had she been a one-night stand, or had he left before he had to face her? How badly she wanted to believe it wasn't the latter.

The strident *buzz* of her alarm clock brought her back to the present. She shut the alarm off and got out of bed. Time enough for reflection later. Right now, she had to get dressed for her first day of work. Wasting no time, she showered, dried her hair, and dressed in brown slacks and a white blouse, what she decided would be proper attire for a veterinarian's receptionist. Dressed, and makeup done to her satisfaction, she went into the kitchen and made coffee. It was a little strange not having to see to Lizzie's morning needs along with her own. However, although she missed her daughter, it was also nice to be able take her time and not have a demanding child to see to and puddles of milk and cereal to mop up.

When the coffeepot had finished its brew cycle, she poured

herself a cup and took a sip. The jolt of caffeine removed any remaining remnants of sleep her shower had left behind, and by the time she heard Cole pull into the driveway twenty minutes later, she was wide awake and ready to face the day, if not the man outside.

THE RIDE TO THE Paws and Claws Clinic was accomplished in a strained silence. It seemed neither of them wanted to talk, fearing that whatever they had to say would segue into talk about the night before.

Cole stopped the car in front of the office and moved the gear shift to Park.

"Thanks," Faith mumbled and started to get out of the car.

"Faith."

She paused, her back to him, and prayed that he was not about to launch into a conversation about the last thing she wanted to discuss. "Yes?"

"I'll pick you up after work and we'll go into Charleston to get your permit. I may be a bit late. I have to drop the squad car off at my house and get my private vehicle. You might want to call Granny Jo and let her know we are going to be late coming to get Lizzie." His tone of voice sounded as though he was conducting an interview with a suspect.

Faith nodded without turning around. "Granny knows. I called her this morning and told her. She's going to feed Lizzie dinner."

"Good." He shifted the car out of Park and into Drive. "See you later."

She'd barely closed the car door when he accelerated out of the parking lot. Tears gathered in her eyes and blurred the brake lights when he paused to check traffic at the end of the driveway. Evidently, she'd been wrong about Cole. He was no better than Sloan. He'd gotten what he'd wanted because she had been stupid enough to let down her guard and give in to her emotions, and now the real Cole had come to the surface. But even as she told herself that, she knew it was just her hurt talking. In her heart, she knew Cole wasn't anything like Sloan.

"Faith?"

Jolted from her problems, Faith looked up to find Hunter Mackenzie standing in the office doorway. "Hi. Hope I'm not late."

"You're right on time." He opened the door wider and ushered her into the clinic. "I have a surgery to perform in a few minutes on a wounded fox that was brought in this morning. Before I get started, I wanted to give you a quick rundown of your duties." He pointed to the chair behind the desk. "You'll be sitting here, and basically, all you'll be doing is answering the phone, making appointments, and then checking them in and pulling their files for me when the patients and owners arrive." He grinned. "Simple. Right?" She nodded. "Any questions?"

"I'm sure I can handle it," Faith said, taking a seat and stowing her purse in the bottom drawer of the desk.

"Well, if you do have any questions, don't be afraid to ask." Hunter walked toward a door behind her. The he stopped and swung back to face her. "By the way, Davy Collins will be in later today to feed the animals. Please tell him I want to speak to him before he starts. I have to give him instructions for feeding the fox I'll be doing surgery on."

She gave him a thumbs-up. "Got it." Then, after Hunter had disappeared into the back room, she made a note to remind herself.

THE MORNING SLIPPED by quickly, filled with calls from Carson residents wanting appointments for their various pets. Bill Keeler needed his blue-tick hound, Rufus, vaccinated so he could take him camping with them. Catherine Daniels made an appointment for her Yorkie, Shasta, to have her ears and teeth cleaned and her nails clipped. Bugs Anderson wanted to know how the fox that he'd brought to Hunter earlier that day was doing. And the list went on, keeping Faith too busy with calls and arriving patients and their owners for her to wallow in thoughts of Cole.

Shortly after three o'clock, the door opened, and Davy Collins came in, accompanied by his wolf Sadie. "Hey, Miss Faith." He glanced around the room. "Where's Miss Rose?"

Faith smiled at the boy's cheery greeting and the smell of bubblegum that seemed to always surround him. "Hello there, Davy. Miss Rose has to take it easy until her baby is born. I'm going to be taking her place until she comes back."

"Sure hope she's okay." He looked toward the house where Rose and Hunter lived on the far side of the clinic property. A worried frown pleated his forehead. Glancing first at Sadie then to Faith, he said, "Sadie usually waits here for me to feed the animals so she doesn't rile them up. They don't really like wolves around them. Miss Rose never minded. Is it okay with you? It's okay if you don't want to have her here. I can always tie her to the tree outside. She won't like it, but it'll only be for a couple of hours." He gasped for air after his prolonged speech.

Faith suppressed a smile. She wasn't nuts about sharing the office with a wolf, however, as long as she had a big solid desk between her and the animal . . . "Sure. Sadie can stay here with me." If it had been okay with Rose, Faith was willing to give it a whirl, even if it did make her a bit nervous.

"Thanks." Davy turned to the wolf and made a slicing motion with his hand. "Sadie, down." With a muffled *thump*, the wolf instantly splayed her big body on the floor, rested her chin on her paws, and watched Davy. Again using his hand, he held up his palm to the big animal. "Stay." Without looking back, he headed for the door. "I'll be getting to work now."

"Davy, Dr. Hunter wants to see you before you start, and I have a question for you."

He turned back. "Okay. I pretty much know all there is to know about most of the animals." His chest swelled. "What do you need to know?"

Grinning at this miniature *animal expert*, Faith leaned forward. "It's nothing about the animals, although I'll certainly keep you in mind if I need to know anything about them. I'm going to have a small birthday party for Lizzie in a few weeks, and I wanted to ask you if you'd like to come."

For a moment, he seemed to be thinking it over, then his eyes brightened and a big smile curved his lips. "You gonna have cake and ice cream?"

"Absolutely."

His grin widened and lit up the room. "Okay. We'll be there. Sadie loves ice cream." Then he zipped past her into the backroom.

Faith laughed. She had a feeling Sadie wasn't the only one who liked ice cream.

THE REMAINDER OF the week passed quickly, and before Faith realized it, it was Friday, and Hunter was locking up the office and hurrying off to check on Rose. Davy had finished his tasks and rode off on his bicycle with Sadie trotting beside him like a faithful dog. Sadie and Faith had made friends, and before the day had ended, Sadie was lying beside the desk, sleeping with her chin resting on the toe of Faith's shoe. Surprisingly, as time passed, Faith found she was no longer the least bit uneasy about a wolf snuggling up to her.

Today would be her first driving lesson. She and Cole had gone to Charleston and gotten her permit and the handbook they gave all new drivers. She'd studied it until she was sure the words would come off the pages. As she'd read it, things came back to her that she'd learned in school. Between the handbook and high school Drivers' Ed, she felt sure she could do this.

As he'd promised, Cole pulled up in his personal car moments after everyone had gone home. He turned off the motor and got out. "Ready for your first lesson?" To Faith's surprise, he was smiling as if the tension of the past few days had never happened. The nerves that had started to tangle in knots at the prospect of his impending arrival began to relax.

"I'm ready." She walked around the car and climbed into the driver's seat.

It felt strange, but at the same time familiar, as memories of her Drivers' Education lessons came slowly back to her. Move the seat forward. Check the rearview mirror. Check the side mirrors. Fasten her seat belt. She turned to Cole to see if he was ready to proceed, but when she saw his long legs folded up almost to his chest to fit in the passenger seat, she laughed out loud.

"Are you gonna be okay?" she asked when she could catch her breath.

He grinned back at her. Her heart fluttered erratically in her chest. "As long as the circulation isn't totally cut off, I should be okay. Besides, I've been in worse predicaments."

Her laughter died when images of the danger he'd faced as a big city detective played through her mind. The idea of Cole being hurt lodged in her throat in a big lump of fear.

He touched her arm lightly. "You okay? You're not nervous, are you?"

Faith quickly cleared her mind and forced herself to concentrate on her driving lesson. "I'm fine. And, no, I'm not nervous at all. I think I remember enough of my Drivers' Ed classes to make this as painless for you as possible."

"Well, then, let's get started."

After shifting into Drive, Faith drove carefully from the parking lot. It surprised her that, after overcoming the urge to constantly adjust the steering wheel, things went rather smoothly. Cole directed her toward the mountain road where there was less traffic. Although it was winding and narrow, she felt safer on those roads than on the town's streets, at least for the next few lessons.

As they rounded a curve not far from her house, she spotted a white SUV parked beside the road. "Is that the same SUV we saw the other day?"

Cole frowned, leaned forward, and studied the car. "I think so. It's got a Georgia plate." He pulled a small notepad from his shirt pocket. "Slow down so I can get the plate number." Faith did as he asked, and he jotted down the series of numbers and letters. As they passed the car, Cole continued to study it.

"Is there something wrong?"

He shook his head. "Probably not. It's just weird that the same car is parked here again." He shrugged. "I'll do a check on it when I get back to the office." He stuck the pad back in his shirt pocket and smiled, relieving the tension that had suddenly filled the car. "Better safe than sorry." Although he'd brushed it off as not important, it bothered Faith that he continued to study the car in the side view mirror after they'd passed it.

AFTER ONLY A week of driving lessons, Cole announced that Faith was ready to take her road test and that he'd made an appointment for her at the DMV in Charleston. He wasn't sure if he was happy that she'd taken one more step toward her complete independence, or upset that his morning and afternoon meetings with her would come to an end. And did this giant step toward independence mean she wouldn't need him anymore?

Although he'd tried to stick to his guns about not allowing his attraction to the beautiful young mother to get serious, his heart had other ideas. He'd gone to bed every night eager to see the dawn because it meant he'd soon have time with Faith. He'd gotten up every morning rife with anticipation for the moment when she'd climb into the car with him for the ride to the vet's clinic.

The more he thought about leaving Carson, Lizzie, and Faith for the job in Atlanta, the more he began to dread the day of his departure. Was he about to make the biggest mistake of his life by leaving? Or was the mistake staying? Aside from the couple of kisses and one night they'd spent together, Faith hadn't indicated that she wanted their relationship to go any farther. Added to all his other doubts was the gnawing suspicion that his attraction to Faith was based more than anything else on his deep-seated need for a family of his own.

He sorted through that question many times until he came to realize that most of his time was spent with Faith, and that Lizzie was rarely present. Although he adored the little girl, he knew if she hadn't been there, his feelings for Faith would have been no different.

There was only one other answer for how he felt. He had

fallen in love with Faith, probably from the first time he'd laid eyes on her in Doc Amos's office.

SEVERAL DAYS AFTER her road test on Friday night, Faith opened her mailbox and removed the few items inside: a circular for the latest sale at Keeler's Market, a flyer advertising a craft fair at the church, and a letter that looked very official from the West Virginia Department of Motor Vehicles. She glanced up at Cole, who had just completed his daily check of her house before allowing her to go inside. Her fingers tightened on the envelope. Her whole body quivered in anticipation of what was in the piece of mail clutched in her hands

"There's a letter from the DMV." She held the envelope out to Cole.

He glanced at the return address. "Well, are you gonna open it?"

Hesitantly, she turned the envelope over and slid her fingernail beneath the corner of the flap. She ran it across, and just before she reached the end, she stopped. So much hinged on this. Independence or continued reliance on Cole for transportation lay inside this envelope.

Her hand shook. "What if I didn't pass?"

Cole's large hand enclosed hers and gave it an encouraging squeeze. "You'll practice some more and then take it again." He released her and stepped back. "Open it."

She pulled the flap loose. Slowly, she slipped the paper from the inside and unfolded it. She closed her eyes and said a little prayer, then looked down at the words. For a moment they swam before her eyes. She blinked and brought them into focus.

"Well?" Cole sounded as anxious as she felt.

"I passed," she said, elation coloring her voice. "I passed." She flung herself into Cole's arms.

He picked her up and twirled her around. "Sweetheart, I am so very proud of you."

He put her back on her feet, and she smiled up at him. "Now, I just have to find a car I can afford. Oh, Cole, thank you.

I couldn't have done it without your help."

"Worry about a car later. Right now, you should be celebrating." Cole took her shoulders in his hands and looked down into her eyes. He brushed her hair off her cheek. "And there's no need to thank me. You're a very strong woman, and you can stand on your own anytime. You don't need me to do that."

Don't I?

Chapter 13

THE NEXT MORNING, Faith heard a car in the driveway. Lizzie ran to the window, pushed the curtain aside, and grinned. "Co!" she cried pointing out the window. "Co!"

Cole? On Saturday? Faith hurried to the door and swung it open. "Do you have your days mixed up? It's Saturday. I don't have to work."

Grinning broadly, Cole strode up on the porch and through the open door. "I know exactly what day it is." He scooped Lizzie up off the floor, kissed her soundly on the cheek, and then cradled her against his broad chest. "I have two reasons for being here today. I brought my car for you to use. I'll use the squad car for now. You can drop me off at my house later today. But before that, I'm taking my two favorite ladies on a picnic to celebrate Mommy passing her driver's test." He tickled Lizzie's tummy, and she giggled. "You want to go on a picnic, sweetie?"

"Go, go, go," Lizzie chanted and pointed at the front door. Then she squirmed until Cole put her down. When her feet hit the floor, she dashed off to her room and came back moments later carrying Fuzzy. "Go." She headed for the door, but Cole intercepted her before she could make her getaway.

Faith wasn't comfortable with this. A picnic just seemed too . . . too intimate. However, if she said no, then Lizzie would go into one of her screaming fits. Faith searched for an excuse to say no and then she'd contend with Lizzie's disappointment afterwards.

"I'm afraid I don't have anything in the house for a picnic." Faith cast a frantic look toward the kitchen. That wasn't really a lie. Her refrigerator was nearly as bare as the cabinets. She'd planned on going grocery shopping today.

"No problem. I have a basket in the car filled with all kinds of goodies from Terri's Tearoom. I even stopped by my sister's and borrowed her Pack 'N Play for this little girl, in case she gets sleepy, and a good supply of red lollipops." He gave Faith an I'm-not-taking-no-for-an-answer look. "Now, if you grab whatever we need for this little lady, we can go."

"Go! Go! Go!"

Lizzie's chanting and Cole's unwavering stare left Faith with no choice. Her argument obviously fell on deaf ears, and no matter what excuse she could devise, neither of them were about to cry *uncle*. Reluctantly, she gathered the items she'd need for her daughter, stuffed them in a diaper bag, and then looked at Cole. "Let's go."

A SHORT TIME later, Cole stopped the car in a place Faith hadn't seen since she was a teenager—Honeymoon Falls, aptly named by Josephine and Earl Hawks after they'd spent their wedding night there years ago. Faith had always loved the falls. It had been her place to escape her mother's strict rules, a place to meet friends and be herself. But even when she had come here alone, it had brought her peace and contentment, a place to dream of a better life far from Carson and her mother.

Faith got Lizzie out of her car seat while Cole unloaded a blanket and the Pack 'N Play. After spreading the blanket, he set up the portable playpen and placed Lizzie and her pal Fuzzy in it. When she pushed out her bottom lip in preparation for a protest, he chucked her under the chin and kissed her cheek.

"Sorry, sweetie, but it's way too dangerous for you to be running around here loose. If you just wait a bit, we'll have lunch ready, and we'll get you out of there. Then later on, your mom and I will take you for a swim."

To Faith's amazement, the pouty lip disappeared, and Lizzie's adoring smile blossomed in its stead. The man definitely had a way with the female sex. But then, Faith already knew that. As hard as she'd tried not to let it happen, she'd gotten caught up in Cole's net of charm, generosity, thoughtfulness, and compassion. However, that didn't mean he had to know that she was as vulnerable to him as any other woman. Nor did it mean she would give in to another night of lovemaking. It had taken most of her life, but she'd finally begun learning from her mistakes, and one of the things she'd learned that was foremost in her mind was no matter how charming he came across, don't jump blindly into a relationship.

Not being able to find someone special brought a wrenching sadness to Faith's soul. She'd always dreamed of having a family and living the happily-ever-after dream that every woman wanted. However, it didn't seem to be in her destiny. Cole had come closer than anyone else in a long time ... then he'd deceived her when he'd deliberately lied about needing a housekeeper. His deception had been a small thing, but when you've lived a life of being let down and believing lies, a small deception could seem to be the size of Hawks Mountain.

Lizzie laughed and roused Faith from her dismal memories. It was a beautiful day in one of her most cherished places in the world, and they were celebrating another big step toward her independence. She should be enjoying it, not raking up the heartbreaks of her life.

By the time she'd pulled herself from her thoughts, Cole had started to unload the goodies from the wicker basket he'd gotten out of the trunk of the car. As she watched, she was once more reminded of his thoughtfulness. He'd remembered from their many conversations while she was learning to drive that her favorite foods were fried chicken and coleslaw. She'd been lucky if Sloan recalled her name, let alone what she preferred to eat.

Lord but it made her sound so stupid to have remained with such a thoughtless, self-centered man. But she knew why she'd done it ... fear of being on her own. When Lizzie came along, the fear intensified. With her daughter's birth, Faith had another life to be responsible for. But when Sloan was no longer in the picture, she'd been left with no choice. Now, since she'd come back to Carson, she knew that she could make it.

"Okay, sweetie." Cole lifted Lizzie from the playpen and seated her between them on the blanket. "Here ya go." He set a paper plate with small pieces of chicken, a few chips, and several carrot sticks in front of her. "Dig in."

Lizzie didn't need a second invitation. She immediately began shoving food in her mouth.

Her mother watched in amazement. "She never eats for me without a lot of coaxing. I should keep you around all the time." The second the words passed her lips, Faith realized how they sounded.

"Is that an invitation?" Cole smiled. From his smug grin, she had a feeling he was enjoying watching her squirm for a bit before he took pity on her and changed the subject. "Want some chicken?"

She eyed him suspiciously, then took the plate he held out, picked up a chicken leg and began eating it without looking at him. She chewed for a while, swallowed, and then looked around. "I always loved this place. I'd forgotten how beautiful and peaceful it is here."

"You've been here before?"

She laughed. "This wasn't just for your older group. It was a favorite place for my crowd to come when I was in high school. If my mother had known how many times I sneaked out of my bedroom window and came here, she would have grounded me for life."

Faith gazed off toward the falls, recalling how strict her mother had been about her daughter enjoying the life of a teenager. Maybe, if Celia Chambers had been a little more flexible, Faith's life would have been drastically different. But then she wouldn't have gotten the greatest gift in the world—Lizzie. She glanced at her daughter and smiled.

"I take it you and your mother didn't get along."

This time, Faith's laughter came out stiff and forced. "You could say that. If it didn't say it was permissible in black and white in her Bible, it was a sin. That tends to put a real kink in a teen's life." She touched the locket beneath her blouse and tried not to think about her mother's visit a few days ago.

"Well, your mother's not here, and we are. We're supposed to be celebrating, so let's forget about anything unpleasant and just have a good day." He smiled. "Deal?"

Faith's heart did a funny little double-time beat. He always knew how to pull her out of her self-pity. She returned his smile. "Deal." She took another bite of the chicken. "Cole, did you ever find out who that car belonged to that was parked on my road?" He shrugged. "Nothing suspicious. Just a Georgia tourist. Probably somebody staying at the lodge and doing some local sightseeing."

"Fower." Both of them turned toward Lizzie, who had lost interest in the food and gotten to her feet. She pointed at a daisy blooming near a large rock, and made a beeline for it. She grabbed the flower's head and pulled on it. "Mine fower."

Cole grinned over Faith's shoulder at the toddler's attempt to pick the flower. Then his face went white. "Lizzie!" Before Faith could turn to see what her daughter was doing, Cole vaulted to his feet. Like an Olympic athlete, he jumped over the food and pushed Faith aside.

The terror in his voice stirred cold chills in Faith. She quickly swiveled on the blanket just in time to see Cole thrust Lizzie aside and fall to the ground. Near his foot, something long and brown streaked off into the nearby bushes. She'd lived in these mountains long enough to recognize the hourglass markings and the pale yellow tail of a copperhead. A chill raced down her spine as she recalled hearing about a small boy being bitten by a copperhead and that he had died from the infected bite.

Not Cole! Please, God. Not Cole!

Lizzie ran to Faith and threw herself into her mother's arms. Faith hugged her close and stared at Cole in frozen terror. He was still lying on the ground clutching his leg and moaning. His audible pain mobilized her. The fear for her daughter, then of the snake, evaporated, and her mind centered on the man writhing on the ground. Quickly, she put Lizzie in the car, and then raced back to Cole.

She knelt beside him. Helplessness overcame her. She could not lose this man. He'd become too much a part of her life. Frantic with fear, she brushed the sweat from his forehead. She knew she should be doing something, but had no idea what.

"What can I do?"

"Take . . . me . . . Doc Amos," he whispered between clenched teeth.

Chapter 14

FAITH STOPPED PACING the waiting room of Doc Amos's office and glanced at Lizzie sleeping peacefully on the leather couch. Satisfied that her daughter was okay, she resumed pacing. Lizzie *was* okay, and it was entirely due to Cole. Without hesitation, he'd put himself between her baby and the snake, probably saving Lizzie's life. Now, he was inside Doc's office fighting for his. The icy fear that had filled her entire being since she'd helped Cole into the car at Honeymoon Falls intensified. What would she do without him? Before she could answer that, a gentle voice cut into her thoughts.

"Honey, you're gonna wear a hole in that floor." Harriet Joseph's tone was soft and sympathetic, but effectively brought Faith's patrolling of the office door to a halt.

Faith moved to Doc's wife's desk, her hands clutched tightly together in front of her. She gnawed nervously on her bottom lip. "What's taking so long?"

Laying aside her pen, Harriet rose and circled the desk. She threw an arm around Faith's shoulders and hugged her. "He'll be fine. Cole's a strong man."

"But they've been in there for so long." Faith threw a worried frown at the closed inner office door, then looked back at Doc's wife.

Harriet checked the clock on the wall above her desk. "Actually, they've only been in there for forty-five minutes. Amos is not one to hurry things when it comes to his doctoring. Now you sit down here by your little one, and I'll get you a cup of tea. I always found that a cup of tea is just the thing when I'm on edge."

Faith allowed Harriet to guide her to the end of the couch where Lizzie slept, unaware that her beloved Cole was in any danger. Once satisfied that Faith was comfortable, Harriet hurried off to get the promised cup of tea.

Hands still clutched in her lap, Faith stared at the closed door. Cole had to be okay. What would she do if anything happened to him?

You'll go on, just like you did after Sloan was killed.

But this wasn't the same. She hadn't loved Sloan, at least not like she—*No!* She couldn't, wouldn't, go there.

THIRTY MINUTES LATER, holding the untouched cup of tea in her cold hands, Faith was still staring at the closed door when it suddenly opened. Cole hobbled through it, supported by a pair of crutches. He looked as if he was suffering from no more than a sprained ankle. Much of the fear that had held her in its icy grasp evaporated.

"You're okay," she whispered, her intense relief evident in her voice.

"Good as new," Cole replied. Then he looked down at the missing lower part of his jeans leg. "Well, at least *I'm* good as new. I can't say as much for my pants."

Fear for Cole's well-being still uppermost in her mind, Faith ignored Cole's attempt at a joke and looked to Doc Amos. "Is he? Good as new I mean?"

Doc Amos guided Cole to a chair and assisted him into it. "He's gonna be fine, Faith. He's just lucky he tangled with a copperhead and not one of our nasty timber rattlesnakes. Unlike rattlers, copperheads are stingy critters. They don't waste their venom on humans. They save it for their edible prey, like mice and small rodents. Added to that was the fact that the bite was more of a glancing blow than a head-on bite." He put a hand on Faith's shoulder. "He may not have even gotten any venom in the wound, but to be safe, I cleaned it out good with a strong antiseptic, gave him a shot of antibiotics, and wrote a prescription for more. He'll have to stay off it for a day or so. And I do mean *off it*." He stared hard at Cole. "However, knowing our illustrious sheriff, I'm going to recommend he get a keeper to glue his rump in a chair and insist he stay there."

Relief flooded through Faith. Cole would be okay. "I'll stay with him," Faith said without thinking.

"No—" Cole's protest was cut short before he could get it all out.

"This is not up for discussion, Sheriff," Faith declared. "It's a weekend, and I don't have to work. I'll stop by my house and pick up everything Lizzie and I will need for a day or two, then we'll get you home and into that chair."

She waited for the man who had suddenly become so important to her to object, but wisely, Cole didn't fight her. He just grinned and murmured, "Yes, ma'am."

Faith told herself she needed to do this because Cole had saved Lizzie's life, and she owed him, big time. But deep inside she knew there was much more to it.

ON THE WAY home, Cole cast side glances at Faith. He hated that she was so worried about him, but contrarily, it also sent warm emotions through him. Would she care this much if her feelings didn't go deeper than friendship? Dared he go there?

Because of his law enforcement training, he'd learned to read people pretty accurately, but Faith baffled him in some ways. She'd returned to Carson determined to establish a life for herself and her daughter, and she'd done a heck of a job at it. In a few short weeks, she'd found a home, a job, and learned to drive. But as strong as she appeared on the outside, Cole worried about how much of that strength was just a wall she'd erected between herself and the world, and, if that wall crumbled, how easily she could be hurt.

Certain that her old emotional wounds had not yet healed over, he'd tread carefully. He'd kept his plan to move to Atlanta from her. Deep inside, he wasn't sure anymore if he wanted to leave Carson. Until he made up his mind, involving Faith in a relationship that might or might not go anywhere was not fair. But every time he saw her, it was getting harder and harder to keep a tight rein on his emotions.

When they arrived at his house, Faith consigned Cole to the couch with strict orders to "Stay put."

Once she got him settled, she called her friend Becky's husband to go to the falls and retrieve their belongings that had gotten left behind in the rush to get Cole to Dr. Amos. She hung up the phone and turned to him. "I'm assuming you have a spare room."

"It's upstairs on the left." He pointed toward the staircase. "But there's no need for you to stay overnight. I can manage."

Faith flashed him her I'm-not-negotiating-this expression, the same one she'd used on him in Keeler's Market the first day he'd taken her grocery shopping and, most recently, in Doc's office. "Doc said for you to keep off that leg for a day or two, and that's what I plan on seeing that you do." He started to protest again, but she sat on the edge of the couch and placed a finger over his lips. "You saved my daughter's life. Let me do this for you."

His body relaxed. "Okay. There's a sofa down here in the den, I'll sleep there so I don't have to climb the stairs. You can take my room if you want and put Lizzie in the spare room."

Faith froze. *His room?* Sleep in *his* bed? Just the thought brought memories of their night of lovemaking slamming into her like an out-of-control semi.

She grabbed at the first excuse that popped into her head. "I'll sleep in the spare room with Lizzie. She might get upset if she wakes up in a strange room."

"Chicken?" Cole flashed a knowing smile at her.

Her heart lurched. Yes. Chicken was exactly the right word for what she was.

TO FAITH'S RELIEF, the rest of the evening and all day Sunday went without any more innuendos from Cole. By Monday morning, they'd settled into a pleasant routine. Faith made the meals and served Cole in the living room so he didn't have to get up on his leg. She and Lizzie ate with him off TV tables his mother had stashed in the hall closet. Faith had changed his bandage and swabbed the wound with the antibiotic solution Doc had provided, and it was looking good. She watched the clock with an eagle eye to make sure he took his meds on time.

Monday morning, she called Hunter, filled him in on what had happened, and told him she wouldn't be in to work until Wednesday. After a Monday afternoon trip to Doc's office, and with his approval, Cole was cleared to go back to work the next day. That evening, Faith fixed spaghetti and meatballs for supper. When she put Lizzie in the highchair Cole kept for his nephew, she took her seat at the table across from Cole. At that moment, how much they looked like any little family sharing an evening meal struck her. But they weren't. And she had to stop dreaming such things. When they'd finished supper, she'd clean up. They'd go to bed, and tomorrow, she'd be back in her little cottage with just Lizzie.

"This is nice," Cole said as if reading her thoughts. "It gets lonely eating alone all the time. It's nice having company."

Afraid to meet his eyes, she looked at her plate and mumbled, "Yes, it is."

"I hate that you'll be going home tomorrow."

She wanted to say she didn't want to leave. She wanted to say how much she'd loved being with him in the last few days, taking care of him. But she didn't. Instead, she smiled and continued to shove food into her dry mouth. She chewed then swallowed. "Will you be okay?"

"Sure. I'll be fine. I've been in worse shape." He reached for a slice of garlic bread, ripped off a small chunk and gave it to Lizzie. "This is delicious. How'd you learn to cook like this?"

She shrugged. "Necessity."

Small talk. What were they not saying? She knew what she was holding back, but what about Cole? What wasn't he saying? And did she really want to know?

WEDNESDAY MORNING came all too soon for Faith. After Cole's last early morning checkup at Doc's, they dropped Lizzie off at Granny Jo's house. Then she and Cole drove by his place so he could pick up his patrol car. He insisted on following her to her home so he could check out her house. When Faith protested, he pointed out that the house had stood empty for three days, so Faith agreed.

She watched him limp up to her front porch, unlock the door, and disappear inside. While she waited, she played the last few days through her mind. A smile curved her lips with the memories she'd stored away like a pirate burying his treasure: cooking for the three of them, *family* dinners, watching Cole play with Lizzie, good-natured arguments over what TV show they'd watch, long talks about things they liked and didn't like. But never, in all that time, had they talked about how they really felt.

As she let the memories cascade through her mind like a slide show, she forgot about Cole checking the house until she heard him shout.

"Faith, you'd better come here."

Disturbed by his alarming tone of voice, Faith scrambled quickly from the car and hurried toward the house. "What's wrong?"

"You'd better see it for yourself." He swung open the door.

Faith stepped inside and looked around. Absolute shock stole her voice.

Chapter 15

FAITH STARED IN frozen silence at her living room. It looked as if a tornado had passed through it. What she could see of her bedroom looked no better. Furniture was overturned. Papers and magazines were strewn about the floor. Drawers were open, their contents spilling out on the floor.

"I don't understand," she whispered. "Who would do this?"

Cole guided her to the couch and seated her, then sat beside her. "Someone was looking for something. Any idea what it would be?"

Faith shook her head, still having trouble forming thoughts and putting them into words.

Looking for what? She certainly had nothing here of value. Still stunned, she stared at the mess all around her. In the far reaches of her mind, she could hear Cole talking.

"Yes, she'll be there, but something's come up, and she's gonna be a bit late. Okay. Thanks, Hunter." Cole put his cell phone away. "I called Hunter and told him you'll be late."

Faith nodded dumbly. "Thanks."

He took her hand. "Faith, remember that white SUV we saw on the road?"

"Yes." *What does that have to do with this mess?*

"I ran the plate, and it belongs to someone from Atlanta. At the time, I figured it was just some tourist who was having car problems."

She frowned. "And now?"

"After this, I'm wondering if I was wrong. Is there anyone in Atlanta who would do this? Maybe someone connected with Sloan? You did say he was into drugs."

The bottom went out of Faith's stomach. Could it be one of Sloan's drug pals who'd invaded her home? But why? "I don't see why. I have nothing here that belongs to Sloan. When we left Atlanta, I only took what belonged to me and Lizzie. As far as I know, all of Sloan's stuff is still in the apartment where I left it."

"But they don't know that."

The thought of that trash breaking in here and contaminating her home pulled Faith from her state of confusion. The numbness that had invaded her senses slowly ebbed. In its place came anger and the sickening sensation of being violated. Even dead, Sloan had found a way to infect her life with fear. She vaulted to her feet and began pacing the room like a caged tiger.

"How dare they! How dare they invade my home and disrespect my privacy. What if Lizzie and I had been here?" Furious tears gathered in her eyes and spilled down her cheeks. She wiped them away with an impatient swipe of her hand. Faith had never known this kind of anger before. It built inside her like a raging fire and ate at her self-control. "My God, what if my baby had been here?"

Cole jumped up and came to her, enfolding her stiff body in his arms. "You weren't here and neither was Lizzie. Don't torture yourself with what ifs, sweetheart." He kissed the top of her head and rocked her until the rage eating at her subsided, and she relaxed against him. "Come on. Let's go in the kitchen, and I'll make us some coffee." With his arm around her and her body tucked close to his, he led her from the living room into the kitchen. "We'll figure this out. I promise. I will never let anything happen to you or Lizzie."

Cole's words and the condition of the kitchen helped Faith calm down a bit. Evidently, whoever did this either hadn't had the time to search the kitchen or had decided that whatever they were looking for wasn't there. It was just as she'd left it the day she walked out to go with Cole on the picnic.

Faith dropped into a chair at the table and buried her face in her hands. She could hear Cole going through the process of making coffee, but her thoughts were ricocheting around in her head, trying to think who could have done this.

Something suddenly occurred to her. Celia. Maybe she was looking for the locket. Although Faith couldn't imagine her mother going to these lengths, it was the only reasonable explanation. But her mother's car wouldn't have a Georgia license plate. Whoever the car belonged to had to be the answer to who had ransacked her home. "Cole, who was that SUV registered to?"

He finished pouring water in the coffeemaker, placed the carafe on the base, and then sat down across from her at the table. He pulled a small notepad from his uniform shirt pocket and flipped it open. "The name was Charles Harrison."

Faith gasped.

"You know him?"

She nodded. "He's my uncle."

This time Cole was the one shocked. "Your uncle?"

"My mother's brother. But I don't know why he would— Oh no!"

Instantly, Cole came alert. His entire demeanor changed. Before her eyes, he became the sheriff, the symbol of law, the man determined to solve this mystery. "What?"

"It was her. It had to be her." Faith dug her grandmother's pendant out of the neck of her blouse, unhooked the clasp and laid it on the table. "My mother was here a while ago asking for this. My grandmother left it to me in her will, and I refused to give it to her. Her exact words when she left were, 'I will get it. Count on it.'"

Cole shook his head. "I can't believe your own mother would do this." He waved his hand at the chaos in the living room. "You're her daughter, for goodness sake. Why in heaven's name would she break into your house and search it?"

"I can believe it." When Cole still looked skeptical, Faith sighed, resigned to telling him about the incident that had happened a few days earlier. "You don't know my mother. For all her Bible pounding, she's a hypocrite." Faith took a deep breath. "When my grandmother died, my mother tore Gramma's house apart looking for the money my grandmother had stashed all over the place. Celia never stopped until she was sure she'd found every last cent. She found enough to buy a car." Faith rose and poured the brewed coffee into two mugs. "If she could desecrate my dead grandmother's house within days of her passing, she'd never let a little thing like me being her daughter stop her from getting what she wants."

Cole sipped his coffee, obviously deep in thought as he digested what Faith had just told him. He set the cup down. "Your grandmother stashed cash around her house? Why?"

Faith giggled, recalling her grandmother's reasoning. "Because she didn't trust banks. Years ago, she and my grandfather fell on hard times, and the bank repossessed their house. From that time on, she said no bank would ever see a cent of her money."

Cole leaned back and shook his head. "I can't believe that Celia would do this just to get her hands on the pendant. What's so special about it that she'd go to these extremes?" He picked up the locket and examined it. "It opens. What's inside?"

"I don't know what it would have to do with all this." Faith took it from him and slipped her fingernail below the tiny catch at the side and flipped the locket open. Inside were two familiar photos. On the left was a picture of her grandmother smiling back at her, love filling her eyes. On the other was a picture of Fuzzy, Lizzie's teddy bear.

Cole turned the locket to look at the photos. "Why would she put a picture of the bear in here?"

Faith smiled and fought back the tears threatening to fall. "My Gramma made Fuzzy especially for me. I was only nine when she gave him to me. She said that I should take care of him, and one day he would take care of me and make all my dreams come true, so she put the picture in there to remind me."

"What did she mean by him taking care of you?"

"She said I'd know when the right time came." Faith shook her head. "After she told me that, I was afraid something would happen to him, so I never played with him. He always sat on my bed." She chuckled. "I think, in my child's mind, I thought he was magic, and I half expected him to come to life when I needed him."

A deep sigh emanated from Cole as he leaned back in his chair and ran his fingers through his hair. "Other than that SUV belonging to your uncle and being parked so close to your house, there's nothing here that points to your mother being the one who did all this. I know it looks that way and there's every reason to believe that it was her, but there's no evidence." He frowned. For a moment, he remained silent. "I can bring her in to the office and question her if you want, but I wouldn't expect too much. She'll most likely deny it, and we can't prove otherwise."

There was just enough of her childhood fear of her mother still remaining in Faith to instill alarm in her. If Celia hadn't done this, and deep down Faith believed she had, she was certain her mother would find a way to make her life a living hell. Right now, Faith had enough on her mind without having to contend with her mother. "No. No. Don't do that. This could have been nothing more than a random burglary." She shrugged. "Maybe some kids looking for something to sell to get money for booze or drugs or whatever."

Cole looked skeptical. "You do realize that this is all speculation."

Faith nodded. "Yes. I know." She also knew exactly how to bring this whole mess to a conclusion.

Chapter 16

LATER THAT NIGHT, Faith sat in the darkened bedroom gazing blindly out the window and trying not to think about Cole sleeping a few feet away in her living room. After finding her house torn apart, he'd insisted on staying with her. Despite any argument she'd made that she'd be fine, he wouldn't budge.

Truth be known, she was glad he was here. It gave her one less thing to worry about and a sense of security and knowing someone cared about her that had become foreign to her until she met Cole. She pushed the events of the day from her mind, but another worry edged its way in to take its place. Money.

Mentally, she reviewed her finances, and the outcome, to say the least, looked bleak. No matter how she'd juggled the numbers, she figured she'd be in the hole for the foreseeable future. Hunter was paying her well for her receptionist services, but with what she owed Doc Amos for rent and utilities, her paycheck didn't stretch very far.

She fingered her grandmother's locket. "Gramma, I sure wish you were here for me to lean on. It seems like for every shovelful of debt I take out of the hole, three more pile back in."

She flipped open the locket and gazed down at its contents: a photo of her grandmother and the photo of a fuzzy bear. "Fuzzy, how are you gonna make my dreams come true? You're just a stuffed toy. Are you gonna pay Doc back or finance Lizzie's birthday party?"

With her piles of debt, Faith couldn't, in good conscience, waste money on a party when she owed Doc so much for all his kindnesses. If there was no party, Lizzie wouldn't know, but Faith would. She would be failing her daughter once again.

At that moment, a mother's love overcame common sense, and Faith made up her mind that even if Doc had to wait for his money, her daughter would have her birthday party. Besides, how much could cake and ice cream cost? After the party was over, she'd make a doubled-up effort to pay off Doc. She was sure he'd understand. Once she'd made her decision, she crawled into bed and slept fitfully.

THE FOLLOWING weekend, Faith had everything in place for Lizzie's birthday party. Hunter's and Rose's twins and Nick's and Becky's son were busy playing with blocks on the living room floor. The adults had gathered in the kitchen.

Despite her tight budget, the party had come together nicely. Granny Jo had made gingerbread cookies for all the children and decorated them with colorful shirts and pants and big icing smiles. Cole had arrived with two cake boxes, one large and one smaller.

After retrieving Lizzie from the living room and carrying her into the kitchen, he opened the big one to reveal the birthday cake in the shape of a teddy bear. "What do you think, sweetie?" He lifted Lizzie so she could see the cake.

Lizzie squealed and pointed at the brown bear cake. "Fussy." It was the one of the few words she came close to pronouncing clearly. She reached for the cake, but Cole rescued it just before her little fingers could wreak havoc on it.

"We have a special cake for you to tear into, sweetheart," he said. Putting Lizzie down, he opened the second box he'd brought into the kitchen. It contained a miniature duplicate of the larger bear cake. "My sister called it a smash cake. She said it's the latest thing for kids' birthday parties. Karen says the process is to set the birthday girl in her highchair, put the cake on the tray, and let her have at it." The expression on Cole's face told Faith that Mr. Neatness was having trouble processing this concept, but he was really enjoying this whole birthday party thing. And if it was for Lizzie, he'd move a mountain.

Faith already knew that Cole never minded lollipop juice on his shirt or sloppy wet kisses from a little girl that thought the sun rose and set in him. In his eyes, Lizzie did no wrong. He genuinely loved the little girl. And that only made it harder for her to fight her growing attraction for him.

Faith took the smash cake and placed it on the table beside the larger one. "She's gonna love this. Thank you, Cole, and please tell Karen thank you for me."

The back door opened, and Davy Collins came in, accompanied by his faithful companion, Sadie. At first Faith wanted to tell him to leave the wolf outside. She was quite comfortable with Sadie, having had her in the office with her on a daily basis. However, she wasn't sure how everyone else would react. But then she realized that she was the only one in the room who showed the least bit of apprehension about the animal joining the celebration.

"It's okay, child." Granny Jo leaned over and patted the wolf's head. "Everyone in Carson has made friends with this big old baby." Sadie licked Granny's hand as if to thank her for her vote of confidence. Then Sadie walked straight to Lizzie and nuzzled her neck.

Lizzie giggled and hugged the wolf. "Dawg!"

"Miss Faith, Lizzie's present is outside. Can I bring it in?" Davy was fairly dancing in place with anticipation.

She smiled at his excitement. "Sure."

Faith had no idea what the present was, but having been around Davy a lot at work, she was prepared for almost anything. He was impulsive, matter-of-fact, sometimes wise beyond his years, and amazing with any animal he came in contact with, and she'd grown to love having him around.

Davy raced out the back door. It slammed noisily behind him. A few moments later, he came back in carrying a white ball of fluff. "It's one of Sadie's babies." He held the puppy out for Faith to take. "It's a boy dog," he added in a very serious tone. "He's two months old, and he still pees inside."

Everyone laughed. Cautiously, Faith lifted the puppy from Davy's hands. A part wolf in her house? "Uh, thank you, Davy."

Faith had to admit the puppy was adorable, white and soft and squirming to get loose. Thankfully, Lizzie was back in the living room playing with Rose's girls. Faith looked at Cole. Her unease must have shown on her face.

He put a hand on her shoulder. As if reading her mind, he said, "It'll be fine. Lizzie will love this. Besides, I'll feel a lot better if you have a dog in the house."

He didn't say why, but Faith knew it was because of the break-in. His concern sent a wave of warm comfort through her. "Okay. Can you get Lizzie, and we'll introduce her to her new friend?"

As Faith had assumed she would, Lizzie was delighted with her new friend. "It's a puppy," Faith explained as she placed the animal in Lizzie's outstretched arms.

Lizzie squealed and hugged the puppy close as he licked her face and nuzzled her neck. "Pup. Mine."

"We have to give him a name." Faith patted the puppy's head.

"Pup," Lizzie announced firmly. "Mine."

Cole kissed Lizzie's cheek. "Pup sounds good to me." Sadie barked. "And it sounds as though his momma approves, too."

Everyone laughed. Davy's gift was the hit of the day. Faith smiled and the last doubt about having spent money she really couldn't afford on this party vanished.

THE FOLLOWING weekend, Cole sat in a meeting in Charleston, but his mind was not on the workshop the FBI agent was giving on the advancements in DNA processing. When it was over, he left the room as soon as he could and headed back to Carson.

Faith was sure her mother had broken into her house, but until Cole saw absolute proof of that, he couldn't rest easy.

He'd spent every night on Faith's couch until Wednesday when she'd insisted she'd be okay and that he needed to go home. Reluctantly agreeing, he'd done as she'd asked, but as a result, had spent the rest of the week in sleepless nights and haunted days.

If anything happened to that woman or her daughter, Cole would not be responsible for what he'd do when he came face to face with the person accountable.

He'd given up denying that he loved Faith, and not because of Lizzie. Yes, he adored the child, but if Faith had been totally alone, Cole would have loved her. And no one messed with the people he loved. In fifth grade, he'd beat the pudding out of a kid who'd called Cole's sheriff father a pig.

Showered and dressed, he carried a cup of coffee into his living room and sat on the couch. On the coffee table was the mail that had accumulated over the time he'd been gone. He set his cup down and picked up the pile of envelopes. Slowly, he thumbed through them, tossing the junk mail aside and collecting the stuff he had to look at in a separate area. About half way through the stack, he found an envelope with the return address of the school in Atlanta where he would begin teaching in the fall.

He opened it and read the words welcoming him to the faculty and setting up a date for him to come for orientation. Leaning back with a heavy sigh, he finally made the decision he'd been putting off for weeks. Going to Atlanta was out. He just couldn't leave Faith. After throwing the letter on the coffee table, he pulled his cell phone out and dialed the number on the letterhead.

SINCE IT WAS THE weekend and Cole had an appointment in Charleston, Faith wouldn't have to be faced with making explanations to him. She took advantage of his absence to do something she'd been planning since her house had been ransacked. Granny Jo had generously agreed to take care of Lizzie for a few hours so Faith could put her plan into action.

After barricading Pup in the kitchen, Faith locked her door and climbed in the car, her destination firmly planted in her mind . . . her mother's. After looking at all the circumstantial evidence, Faith was certain it had been her mother in the house. Faith was also certain her mother had been looking for the locket, and she suspected it wasn't the first time either. Faith recalled other times when she could find no logical explanation for things being out of place or her front door left ajar. At the time, she'd dismissed them as something either she or Lizzie had done, but now she didn't believe that.

The time had come to face her mother.

When she arrived at her mother's, both her father's car and her mother's car were in the driveway. The house looked no different than it had when Faith had walked out, suitcase in hand, a week after her eighteenth birthday. The paint was snowy white, the lawn was mowed and trimmed within an inch of its life, and the tops of the shrubs were shaved so flat that they could have been used as a table. She could hear the low hum of the lawn mower where her father was probably mowing the grass behind the house.

To an outsider, it was a neat, suburban home. To Faith, it was proof that her father was still firmly under her mother's demanding thumb. Saturdays were for yard work and house-cleaning. While her father had toiled outside, and while her friends were out enjoying the day, Faith had labored inside under her mother's critical eye. Sundays were for God, according to her mother. No work was done except to cook Sunday dinner after going to church. The afternoon was spent reading the Bible and praying for forgiveness for all the sins her mother was more than happy to point out for both Faith and her father. It never escaped Faith's notice that their list of sins was always much longer than Celia's.

A neighbor's dog barked, rousing Faith from her childhood memories. Taking a deep fortifying breath, she grabbed her purse and climbed from the car. By the time she'd reached the front porch, she had begun second-guessing herself. She could turn around now and go home, and Celia would never know she'd been there.

Or you can pull up your big girl pants and finally face her.

She raised her fist and knocked.

Chapter 17

FAITH KNOCKED ON her mother's front door and waited. When no one answered, she knocked again. As she knocked for a third time, she reluctantly decided that if no one answered this time, she'd leave. Then she heard the distinctive *click* of her mother's sensible shoes on the hall floor. Moments later, the door opened.

Celia Chambers stared at her. Quickly, her mother's look of surprise changed to the familiar frown Faith had seen many times while growing up. "Faith." Her voice was cold and sounded as though she was talking to an unwelcome door-to-door salesman.

"Hello, Mother." Faith tamped down her disappointment at her mother's cool greeting. Annoyance that her mother could still hurt her after all these years helped her screw up the courage to proceed with her plan, courage that without knowing it, Cole had helped her recognize in herself. "We need to talk."

Celia said nothing. She stepped aside and waved her hand as a signal for Faith to enter the house. Once inside, her mother walked around her and into the pristine living room, obviously expecting Faith to follow. Again, without words, Celia waved her hand at the couch as a sign for Faith to sit. The silence surprised Faith. Her mother had never been at a loss for words before.

"So," Celia seated herself in the wing chair facing Faith and folded her hands primly in her lap, "what is it we need to talk about? Dare I hope you've seen the error of your ways, and you've come to beg my forgiveness?"

As Faith gathered her thoughts, she ignored her mother's jibe and looked around the room she'd spent so many hours in. Nothing had changed. It was if she'd walked out this morning.

Her mother's Bible lay on the coffee table as it always had. The furniture glowed, and the drapes were drawn, shutting out the bright sunlight so it wouldn't fade the upholstery while they closed out the sinful world beyond. Framed photos of the Chambers and Harrison families stood like soldiers awaiting inspection on the sideboard. Noticeably missing were any pictures of Faith. Pain Faith didn't want to acknowledge arrowed through her. Her mother had truly removed her from her life.

Unable to put it off any longer, Faith straightened her shoulders and plunged in. "We need to talk about your visit to my house."

Celia's eyebrow shot up. "Why? I thought we had adequately covered that by the time I left."

"Not that visit, Mother. I mean your visit while I wasn't home." Her mother's obvious discomfort surprised Faith. But the expression came and went so quickly, Faith questioned if it had actually been there, or if she had wished it.

Celia smoothed the material of her dress over her knees, raised her chin, and glared at her daughter. "I'm sure I don't know what you're talking about."

Anger boiled inside Faith, but she kept it in check. "Don't insult my intelligence or yours by denying it, Mother. You drove Uncle Charles's car to my house, broke in, and ransacked it."

Celia sprang to her feet. "I think you should leave."

A bit of the anger seeped out. "Sit down, Mother," she said stiffly. Shocked that she'd stood up to her mother, Faith squared her shoulders. She had to admit, asserting herself felt good, empowering. For once, she was not going to be the victim. "The only reason I haven't gone to the authorities is because you're my mother, and I'm hoping we can settle this between us."

The threat of the police took the wind out of Celia's sails. She sank back down on the chair, her complexion suddenly a little paler.

Faith felt a slight pang of compassion for the woman who had never made excuses for her behavior in her life. Celia had ruled her house with an iron hand. Her daughter had succumbed to Celia's will because she was her mother. Her husband had caved because he was weak. Now Celia was on the receiving end of the accusing finger.

"You're my mother, and I've tried to love you, but you've never made it easy. I know I've made mistakes. I'm not perfect, Mother, but neither are you. When you broke into my house, you stepped over the line. What I want to know is why?"

The woman who had made Faith's life a living hell stared defiantly at her. "I have no idea what you're talking about."

The anger Faith had kept tamped down fought harder for recognition. She gripped her hands together tightly in her lap and took several deep breaths. Why did she think she could get her mother to admit what she'd done? This was a woman who had never been wrong in her life, at least not in her own eyes. She claimed to live by the Good Book, but both Faith and her father knew that wasn't true.

Faith stood. "I was going to give you Gramma's locket if you'd been honest and admitted what you'd done. But since you won't, the locket will be passed down to my daughter. Your granddaughter, whether or not you recognize her as such." She paused to gather her tangled emotions. "I feel sorry for you, Mother. You'll never know that beautiful little girl. You'll never feel her arms wrapped around your neck or be the recipient of her sweet kisses." She walked to the doorway and stopped. "If you ever change your mind and can call Lizzie your grand-daughter and love her like Gramma loved me, you'll be welcome in our home. Until then, if you ever enter my house again without my permission, I *will* call the police."

Celia vaulted to her feet, her face red and twisted with rage. She raised her hand, and pointed her finger at Faith. "Don't threaten me, girl. You will regret it."

Faith walked out the front door, down the porch steps, and then climbed into her car. Once she settled back in the seat, her body shook uncontrollably with the remnants of her anger, undeniable relief, and a tangle of emotions she couldn't even put a name to. At the same time, the huge weight that had been sitting on her soul lifted. She'd resigned herself to the fact that she couldn't change her mother. Faith could only control how she reacted to Celia, bless her, and set her free.

BY THE TIME FAITH had picked up Lizzie from Granny Jo's, walked Pup, fed Lizzie, and gotten her bedded down for her afternoon nap, she was washed out. No sooner had she collapsed in one of the living room chairs than she heard a car in the driveway. Expecting it to be Cole, and oddly eager to share her day with him, she opened the door before he had a chance to knock.

But she didn't recognize the car. However, she did recognize the man who got out of it. Her heart skipped several beats. To Faith's utter surprise, her father was walking across the lawn toward her.

"D . . . Daddy?" The word was forced from her suddenly dry throat. Not knowing what to expect, she waited, her nerves as tight as a bowstring.

Horace Chambers stopped a few feet away and stared at her. He'd aged, but his still-handsome face creased in a tentative smile. "Hi, Princess. Am I welcome here?"

Relief flooded her. Faith ran into his arms. "You're always welcome here, Daddy." Stepping back, she took his hand and led him toward the house. "Please come inside."

He flung his arm around her shoulder as they walked together. Faith guided him to the living room and sat beside him on the couch, her hand still clutched in his. She stared at him, unable to believe he was actually here. "Does Mother know you came here?"

He nodded. "Yes, I told her I was going to see my daughter and granddaughter, and if she didn't like it, she would just have to learn to live with it."

Faith couldn't believe her ears. She'd never known her father to stand up to her mother. In all the years of their relationship, her easy-going father had always allowed her mother to rule the roost, while he stayed quietly in the background. Why this sudden change?

"Oh," was all she could say.

He squeezed her hand. "I heard what went on between the two of you when you came to the house. First of all, she never told me there was a grandchild. If she'd had her way, I would have gone through life never knowing. I know I haven't always been the leader in our relationship, but I couldn't have that. I want to meet my granddaughter." He looked around them. "Where is she?"

"Sleeping, but she'll be awake before too long. If not, I'll wake her up to meet her grandfather." Faith paused then asked the one question she needed an answer to just to ease her own mind. "Did Mother break into my house, Daddy?"

He paused for several moments before answering. "Truthfully, I don't know for sure. I do know she borrowed her brother's car when he came to visit that day. I never saw a reason for it. Hers was working just fine. When she came home, she was all aflutter. Her hair was messed up, and she was breathing hard. She wouldn't tell me why. After your visit, I put two and two together."

That confirmed for Faith what she already knew in her heart. "Why would she do it?"

Her father shrugged. "I don't know that either. I know she's always felt that she never found all the money your grandmother had hidden around the house."

"But why would she expect to find it here? The only things in this house that belong to me are Lizzie, her few toys, and our clothing."

Before Horace could answer, a cry came from the bedroom. "Momma! Pup! Momma! Pup!"

Her father's grin lit up the room. "Sounds like my granddaughter's awake."

Fifth laughed, and then stood. "Yes, she does make herself heard. I'll go get her."

When she entered Lizzie's room, her daughter was hanging over the crib rail trying to reach Pup. "No, Pup! No!"

Lizzie had thrown Fuzzy out of the crib and now the dog was lying on the floor happily chewing on the bear's ear. It wasn't the first time Pup had commandeered the bear as a chew toy. Ever since he'd come to live with them, Faith had been forced to rescue the toy from the sharp puppy teeth.

"Pup, that's not yours." Faith snatched Lizzie's favorite toy from the puppy and gave it to her daughter.

Lizzie cuddled it close. "Bad Pup!"

"Yes, he's a bad pup," Faith told Lizzie as she carried her child into the living room to meet her grandfather. "Lizzie, this is your Papa."

Lizzie stared at Horace, her eyes wide. "Papa." Then she thrust the bear toward him. "Fussy. Bad Pup."

He gazed at the child, his face wreathed in smiles. "She's beautiful. May I hold her?" As Faith transferred her daughter to her father's waiting arms, he stared down at the bear. "Good grief, is that your old bear, Faith?" Faith nodded. "I would have thought it fell apart years ago."

Fait laughed and tried to tamp down her shock at how easily Lizzie went to Horace. Cole had been the only other man to break through her dislike of males. "Well, it seems that if Pup has anything to do with it, its life expectancy is in serious question."

"Bad Pup," Lizzie chimed in at the mention of her dog's name.

"He certainly is a bad pup," Horace said. He sat down on the couch and settled Lizzie on his lap. "I'm sure your mommy will make sure he doesn't eat such a fine upstanding bear."

Faith sat in the chair across from them and watched as her father and daughter became acquainted. A wave of contentment spread through her like a summer breeze warming the earth of Hawks Mountain.

Finally, her life was settling down. For the first time, she felt that perhaps this move back home wasn't a mistake after all.

Suddenly, the door burst open.

Chapter 18

COLE STORMED THROUGH Faith's front door and stopped dead. He stared at the man holding Lizzie. This was not what Cole had expected. He immediately recognized the man. "Horace?"

Obviously too astonished to speak, Horace nodded and pulled Lizzie closer.

"Co!" Lizzie yelled.

Faith vaulted to her feet, mouth agape. "Cole? What is it?"

Horribly embarrassed, Cole's entire body relaxed. "I'm sorry, Faith. I saw the strange car in the driveway," he waved a hand toward Horace's car, "and considering what's been going on around here lately, I naturally—"

"Enough." Faith stopped him with a raised hand and a smile. "I think your foot is far enough in your mouth."

Cole just nodded his agreement. How could he possible explain to her the abject fear that had gripped him when he saw the strange car? Even now that he knew there was no threat to either Lizzie or Faith, his heartbeat still drummed against his chest.

He combed his hand through his hair and took a step out the door. "I'm sorry. I'll . . . I'll just be going."

"No, please don't go." Faith took his arm, closed the door, and drew him into the room. "My dad came to meet his granddaughter."

Cole leaned over and kissed Lizzie's cheek. "She's a real sweetheart, isn't she, sir?"

Horace beamed. "That she is, Sheriff."

"Co!" Lizzie held up her bear. "Fussy. Bad Pup."

Cole turned to Faith for a translation.

"Pup was trying to eat Fuzzy. But I rescued him." She

smiled at her daughter. "That's my claim to fame. Rescuer of stuffed animals."

Horace didn't seem to notice, but Cole caught the tone of defeat in Faith's voice. When would she realize how strong she was? It hurt his heart to see her lack of understanding of what a wonderful person she was, how compassionate, and gentle.

Horace stood and placed Lizzie on the floor. "I have to be going. Celia will have supper ready." He kissed Faith's cheek. "I love you, Princess, and I hope it'll be okay if I come back again."

"Always, Daddy." Tears glistened in her eyes. "Always."

That Faith had reconnected with her father brought peace to Cole. Family was very important. Lizzie needed her grandfather, and Faith needed her father.

"Good bye, Lizzie. Take good care of Fuzzy bear." He leaned down and kissed the little girl's cheek, straightened, kissed and hugged Faith, and then extended his hand to Cole. "Take good care of my girls."

Cole gave Horace's hand a firm shake. "I will, sir. Count on it." As he watched Horace walk toward his car, Cole had to wonder how such a good man had gotten paired up with Celia Chambers. They were as different as night and day. Faith came to stand beside him and, without thinking about it, he put his arm around her and pulled her snugly against his side. "He's a good man, Faith."

"Yes, he is." She sighed and looked up at him and smiled that smile that turned his insides to mush. "I was about to make supper. Why don't you stay? Consider it payment for playing my knight in shining armor."

"No."

Faith stared at him. "No?"

"You and Lizzie are coming to my house for supper."

She smiled. "You can cook?"

He laughed. "I'm a bachelor, Faith. I either cook or starve." Suddenly turning serious, he cupped her face. "Besides, it'll be nice to look up and see you sitting across the table from me."

It wasn't the words Cole said, but the way he said them that gave Faith reason to hope he would one day return her love and that there was a glimmer of hope for a tomorrow with him.

MAKING DINNER HAD turned into a joint operation. Faith made a meatloaf while Cole peeled potatoes and made a salad. Her earlier spark of hope for them grew as they worked side by side in his kitchen. Dinner was equally as enjoyable. For the first time in her life, Faith felt like she was part of something. Aware that her imagination was working overtime, she ignored her mind's warnings and basked in the moment. She loved this man, and if there was a hope in the world that they could ever have a life together, she was not about to screw it up with her doubts and what ifs.

After giving Lizzie a bath and putting her to bed in the Pack 'N Play in Cole's spare room, Cole and Faith finished the dishes, and then retired to the living room.

Cole leaned back on the couch and emitted a contented sigh. "That's the best meatloaf I've ever had. You never did tell me where you learned to cook like that. And I'm not going to accept 'out of necessity' for an answer this time."

The aura of happiness she'd experienced during supper still enveloped Faith. She settled in beside him. "When I was a kid, my mother made sure I helped in the kitchen, and I picked up on some of her recipes."

Shifting so he faced her, Cole frowned. "So do you still think it was your mother who broke into your house?"

Faith really didn't want a discussion of her mother to infringe on what so far had been a really pleasant evening, but Cole waited for an answer. "Yes, even more so now than I was before. My dad said some things that convinced me it was her."

"Really? What things?"

Faith sat up. "Cole, I don't want to talk about my mother."

He seemed to consider it for a moment, and then nodded. "I know you probably don't, but I need to make sure that it is your mother and not some of Sloan's druggie friends." He took her by the shoulders. "You have no idea how scared I was when I saw that strange car in your driveway."

She could see the shadow of residual fear in his expression. Not until that moment did she fully realize how frightened he'd been. She cupped his cheek in her palm. "There's no need for you to worry." She gave in, hoping to get past this conversation, and told him what her father had said about her mother, and how she'd looked on the day of the incident. "He didn't say so, but I got the impression he thought it was Mother who broke into my house."

"Thank God." Cole pulled her into his arms and held her so tight she wondered if he'd smother her. Then he kissed her forehead. "I don't know what I'd do if anything happened to you or Lizzie." He pulled back far enough to look into her eyes. "I care about you both too much to allow anything to happen to either one of you."

His words gave rise to a burst of happiness that took her breath away. Faith shook her head. "Nothing's going to happen to us. Promise."

He didn't look as if he believed her, but he nodded and flashed a forced smile. "Okay." He stood. "The coffee should be ready by now." He ran his hand over her cheek, and then disappeared into the kitchen.

Faith's gaze followed him until he disappeared through the kitchen doorway. *Cared about them.* The echo of those three words elated Faith. Was it possible his caring could grow to love?

She looked around the cozy living room, and then her gaze dropped to the floor. A piece of paper that had fallen from the coffee table caught her eye. She picked it up, and her gaze went to the bold black words in the letterhead. Why would Cole be getting a letter from a high school in Atlanta?

Although she knew it was none of her business, her curiosity got the best of her, and she read the first sentence.

Dear Mr. Ainsley,

We are happy to welcome you to our faculty. This letter is to inform you that we will be holding an orientation luncheon for the new faculty members on . . .

Faith stopped reading and dropped the paper as if it was on fire. It couldn't have hurt more if she'd been hit in the stomach with a two by four. Cole was leaving Carson. She couldn't believe it. How could he do this to her? How could he become so much a part of her and Lizzie's lives knowing he would be walking away? Why hadn't he told her?

She held back hurt, angry tears. She would not shed one more drop for a man who couldn't be trusted. And that was the bottom line . . . allowing that trust and her dream of a bright tomorrow to see the light of day again. The one thing she'd sworn not to do was trust blindly, and she'd done it anyway.

She had to get out of here. Quickly, she went to the spare room and got Lizzie. Her confused daughter whimpered and snuggled close to her mother.

"It's okay, baby. Go back to sleep. We're going home."

As she entered the living room, Cole emerged from the kitchen carrying a tray with cups, a coffee carafe and sugar and creamer. "Did she wake up?"

Faith wasn't ready to face a confrontation with Cole. Her nerves were stretched to the breaking point, and she was not sure what she'd say. "Yes," she lied, "she's a little warm, and I think I should get her home and give her an aspirin."

Cole looked concerned but gave her no argument. He set the tray on the table. For a moment, he stared down at the letter lying next to it. Then he looked at Faith. She could tell by the expression on his face that he knew she'd seen the letter. "Let me explain."

The anger boiling inside her nearly prevented Faith from speaking, but she forced the words past her lips. "You can't say anything I'd believe. Just take us home." She turned and walked out the door.

WHEN, AFTER A silent, tension-filled ride, they reached Faith's house, she never gave Cole a chance to say anything. She retrieved Lizzie from her car seat and almost ran into the house. Inside, she put Lizzie to bed and then sat on the couch in the dark and allowed the tears to fall.

Cole had tried to talk to her in the car, but she'd turned a deaf ear to him. After all, what could he say that would explain him keeping his departure from Carson a secret from her? Letting her believe he cared? Nothing. He'd betrayed her trust. Period. The pain of his lie by omission cut so deep Faith doubled over in emotional agony.

Then she straightened and brushed the moisture from her cheeks. In truth, she had no one but herself to blame for this. Wasn't it her own fault that she'd read more into their relationship than had been there? He'd helped her settle in when she was newly back in town. He'd protected them, especially Lizzie. He'd seen that they were watched over when the break-ins began. Nothing romantic about it. Nothing that one friend wouldn't have done for another friend. Even that one night of lovemaking could have been nothing more than two people releasing pent-up physical needs. As usual, it was her own fantasizing that had led her to believe there was more there than actually was. That she had fallen in love with Cole did not mean he felt the same.

When would she learn? When would she realize that there were no tomorrows for her? Only the requirement to get through today.

A noise in the kitchen drew her attention from her thoughts. Not until then did she remember the dog. Poor Pup was probably walking cross-legged by now. She dragged herself into the kitchen, and then flipped on the light.

Pup sat in the corner with that look that a dog gets when he knows he's done something very wrong. Scattered over the floor were pieces of what once had been Fuzzy bear along with numerous puffs of cotton innards. Faith's heart sunk. Lizzie would be inconsolable. How could they have left Fuzzy behind to be ravaged by a playful puppy?

"Pup, want have you done?"

Pup dropped his head, laid back his ears, and tucked his tail between his legs. If he could talk, she was sure he'd be saying what was written in his soulful brown eyes. *I'm sorry. Please don't be mad at me.*

Just what she needed to cap off the day. She didn't have the strength to reprimand him. "Come on. Let's take a walk, then I'll see what I can do to bring Fuzzy back to life before your little friend wakes up and throws a tantrum."

As soon as Pup had done his business, Faith hurried him back inside, cleaned the remnants of Fuzzy up and placed them on the couch, then barricaded Pup in the kitchen with his food dish. Once the dog was safely confined, Faith retrieved the sewing kit from the cabinet in the living room and settled on the couch to begin the repair job.

Fuzzy had held up well over the years. As a child, Faith had never played with him and had instead kept him ensconced on her bed. Lizzie, on the other hand, carried him everywhere, and he was beginning to show some wear. Now, the poor thing was in pieces. But in a way, Faith was grateful to Pup for the distraction. Concentrating on reassembling the toy would keep her mind off her heartache.

Thankfully, the dog had just torn off the bear's appendages and ripped the insides from them. When she'd gathered the stuffing into a pile, she had to wonder how one medium-sized bear could hold this much cotton and if she would be able to get it all back inside him. If Pup had chewed up the dislodged parts, she wasn't sure she'd have been able to save Fuzzy at all. Aside from a few small tears in the bear's torso from Pup's sharp puppy teeth, most of the bear's parts were intact.

Hours later, Faith had the ears, head, body, and arms secured. All she had left to do was stuff and sew on the legs, and Fuzzy would be Fuzzy again. He might be a little worse off for his run-in with Pup, but Lizzie wouldn't notice that as long as she had her precious toy back.

When she started pinning the first leg in its respective spot, she realized one leg was missing. She searched through the stuffing and all around the couch. Finding nothing, she concluded it must be somewhere in the kitchen. Laying the bear aside, she went to find its missing limb. She moved the barricade, flipped on the light, and looked around, but saw nothing. Getting down on her knees, she ran her hand under the overhang at the bottom of the cabinets. Along with more stuffing, she finally got hold of the elusive body part. To make sure she had all the cotton, she continued to feel under the cabinet lip.

She'd just about decided she had everything when she felt something odd. Grabbing it, she pulled it out. When she looked down at what she held in her hand, she gasped.

Chapter 19

FAITH GAPED DOWN at a thick roll of money held together by a rubber band. Her hand began to shake. Her knees gave way. She sank back on her rump. The top bill was a hundred dollar denomination with the edge showing telltale marks of puppy teeth. She was almost afraid to release the roll to see what the other bills were.

She pulled herself to her feet and then returned to the couch in the living room, still staring at what she'd found and trying to comprehend exactly what she had and how it had gotten in her kitchen. Certainly, if it had been there all along, she would have found it when she'd swept the floor. From the tufts of stuffing clinging to the rubber bad, she assumed the money had come from inside the bear. And there was only two people she could think of who would have access to that amount of money—her grandmother and . . . Sloan Phillips.

Out of nowhere, a vision that had been burned in her memory flashed through Faith's mind of the Atlanta police standing in her doorway telling her Sloan had been killed because he'd held out on his drug buddies. Had Sloan hidden the money in Lizzie's bear? Is that why they killed him? Had her mother really been telling the truth about not searching her house? Had it been Sloan's drug cohorts all along? What would she do if they came back while she and Lizzie were home alone?

The longer she thought about it, the more frightened she became. A lump of intense fear settled in her stomach in a large, icy ball. Cold sweat beaded her forehead and coated her palms. Her hand shook so hard she dropped the roll of money. It rolled across the floor, and she stared at it as though it was a poisonous snake.

Without thinking, she reached for her cell phone and dialed

Cole's number. When he answered, she fairly screamed. "I need you, now!"

WITH FAITH'S TERRIFIED voice echoing through his very soul, Cole broke every speed limit as he sped toward Faith's house. Scenarios of why she needed him tumbled through his thoughts. Was Lizzie sick? Had she hurt herself? Was Faith hurt? Had her mother broken in again? He dismissed the last thought. Faith was a strong woman. She could handle her mother. It had to be something worse. He jammed his foot down harder on the gas pedal.

Minutes later, the squad car careened into the driveway, and Cole had barely turned off the engine before bolting from the car and racing toward the house. He had one foot on the porch when the door opened, and Faith launched herself into his arms.

"What is it? Talk to me, Faith." He cradled her close and fought to keep the fear from his voice.

She buried her face in his chest and babbled incoherently. "Puppy . . . Fuzzy . . . money . . . Lizzie."

Her body shook against his and not until he felt the moisture seeping into his shirt did he realize she was sobbing. "Sweetheart, calm down. I don't understand what you're saying. Is Lizzie okay?"

She nodded.

"Are you okay?"

Again, she nodded.

Still holding her close, and relieved that neither she nor Lizzie were hurt, he guided her back into the house and then toward the couch. When he saw the mess on the sofa, he stopped. He recognized it immediately as Fuzzy, Lizzie's treasured companion. But why would the bear being torn up upset Faith this much? Then she pointed at the roll of bills lying on the floor.

After seating Faith on the sofa, Cole picked up the money. The size of the roll and the one-hundred bill on top took Cole's breath away. He guessed that, if all the bills were of the same denomination, there had to be thousands of dollars in that roll. He held the roll out to Faith. "Where did this come from?"

She hiccupped, swiped at her wet cheeks, and took an unsteady breath. "Fuzzy." Then she haltingly spilled out the story of what had happened since she got home. When she'd finished her tale, she finally took a deep breath and said, "I think I know how it got there."

Cole sat beside her. "How?"

"Sloan's drug money. I think he put it inside the teddy bear because he figured no one would guess it would be there, but he got killed before he could do anything with it." She sighed. "He was holding out on them. That's why they killed him."

Wow! That was the very last thing Sloan expected to hear, but having worked in a big city police force, he'd seen stranger things.

Suddenly, Faith stood and began pacing the floor. "Damn him! How could he put Lizzie and me in danger like this? How could he be so thoughtless?" Then she laughed mirthlessly. "Not that he ever gave much thought to us anyway."

Cole watched her pace as she poured out an indictment of Sloan Phillips. She was angry and that was much better than the emotional wreck he'd found when he first got there. While he processed all this, he allowed her to fume for a few more minutes.

He finally understood where her fear had come from. How could he alleviate her anxiety? Then he had an idea. He got up and took her in his arms. "Honey, you need to calm down so we can talk this out." He lifted her chin with his finger, kissed her lips lightly, and then turned her loose. "I need to make a phone call. Why don't you make us some coffee?"

Her anger evidently burned out, she nodded and went into the kitchen. Cole stared after her for a few moments. He wanted to grab her and wrap her in his arms to protect her from every bad thing in the world. He wanted to kiss her—

Be honest with yourself. You want to make love to her until the sun comes up.

He swore softly under his breath, disgusted with himself for very possibly screwing up the best thing that had ever happen to him. With one last glance toward the kitchen, he pulled his cell phone from his pocket, and then punched in the number of his friend at the Atlanta PD.

FAITH COMPLETED the mindless task of preparing coffee. She pushed the "on" button and stared unseeing at the machine as it gurgled and sputtered through the brewing process. Although she felt better now that Cole was here with her, cold dread that Sloan's sins had come back to haunt her still sent chills coursing over her. In her heart, she knew she would never have peace of mind until she was certain that there was no more spill-over from Sloan's criminal lifestyle. But she feared that time would never come.

All the what-ifs that had troubled her before Cole got there raced around in her mind again. Absolutely nothing proved that Sloan had stashed the money in the bear, but she couldn't get the idea out of her head.

Faith realized that her panic was clouding her mind and paralyzing her thought process. She tried to clear it away so she could make some sense out of all this. Closing her eyes, she counted slowly to ten. It helped some, but the tantalizing questions were still there and without answers.

"Coffee ready?"

Cole's voice roused her from her mental prison. She checked the pot and realized that it had finished the brewing process already. How long had she been standing here lost in her frightening reflections? "Yes. Sit down, and I'll get the cups."

When they were both settled side by side at the table with their coffee, Faith cupped her hands around the hot mug. She found the sting of the heated ceramic against her palms oddly soothing. Cole pulled her hands from the mug and covered them with his. The feel of his skin on hers washed away the remaining fear. How did this man have the power to bring her a serenity that she'd never known before in her life?

Because you love him.

"Listen to me." He squeezed her hands gently, and she

136

raised her gaze to meet his captivating eyes. "I just called a friend of mine on the Atlanta PD Homicide Division. I should have done it sooner, but you were so sure your mother was the one who had broken into your house, that I dismissed Sloan's buddies. I apologize for that."

Faith held her breath for what was to come next. Would this confirm her worst fears?

Obviously having seen the fright return to her expression, Cole smiled and ran a finger over her cheek. "It's good news, sweetheart. I asked him to check on Sloan's case, and he said it was closed. They caught the guys who killed Sloan a couple of weeks after the murder. They are, as we speak, enjoying the hospitality of the Atlanta jail and awaiting trial."

Faith felt the strength slip from her body. She felt as if she'd been standing on the edge of a cliff and Cole had pulled her back to safety.

"Thanks," was all she could manage. "So, if it wasn't them, where did it—" With the specter of drug dealers ready to do harm to her or Lizzie to get their money lifted, Faith's head cleared and practical reasoning took over.

If it wasn't Sloan's buddies, then who? Suddenly, her second choice came flashing to mind. "Of course. It makes perfect sense." She shook her head in wonder.

Cole looked alarmed. "What?"

She sat back in her chair, smiled, and then looked at Cole. "I think I know where the money came from." She hesitated, certain that Cole would think she'd gone over the edge after she said it. "My grandmother put it there."

"Your grandmother?" He sounded as shocked as she had been when she found the roll of bills. And she couldn't blame him. It wasn't something a person heard every day. Deep frown lines creased his forehead. "I don't understand."

She swung around in her chair to face him squarely. "Remember I told you my grandmother made Fuzzy for me and that she told me he would look after me even after she was gone?" Cole nodded. "Well, put that together with her habit of hiding money, and it makes perfect sense." The look of incredulity on his face pushed her to rush on with more details. "And don't forget the picture of the bear in my locket. I think it was my grandmother's idea of a hint."

His frown deepened. "If all that's true, why didn't she just tell you the money was inside the bear?"

Faith laughed. "I was nine years old. Why would she tell a child where a wad of cash was hidden? Besides, she never really had the chance. She passed away a few weeks after she gave me the bear."

Cole leaned back in the chair and chuckled. "I've never heard anything this crazy before." He scratched his head. "But, right now, it's the only thing that comes close to making any kind of sense."

Faith took a sip of her lukewarm coffee. "If you knew Gramma Harrison, you'd understand. This is so like her."

Cole finished his coffee and stood. "Well, now that the mystery seems to be solved, and if you're sure you're okay, I guess I'd better go home."

A little voice inside Faith was telling her not to let him go. *Do not let him walk away. Tell him you are not okay. Tell him you need his strength every day, all day. Tell him you want to talk about the letter from the high school. Tell him you want him to stay forever. Tell him you love him.*

But she said none of these. After what she'd been through in the last few hours, she wasn't sure her emotions could stand that conversation if it ended with losing him. Instead, she thanked him for coming, walked him to the door, and then watched him drive away.

As she stared at the red glow of the squad car's taillights disappearing around the bend, she asked herself one more question. *Haven't you lost him already by not telling him all those things?*

COLE STOPPED THE car for the fourth time on the mountain road. Each time, his intention had been to turn the car around and go back to Faith's to make her listen to his explanation about that letter. Each time, he chickened out, sure that she'd made up her mind that he couldn't be trusted.

His insides were in turmoil, and his temples were throbbing. It had been easier to walk away from a budding career in law enforcement than it had been to walk out of her house tonight. When he'd announced he was leaving, he had prayed she tell him to stay, but she hadn't. More than anything, he'd wanted to take her in his arms, tell her he wasn't going anywhere, and that he loved her more than his next breath.

So why didn't you?

"Because I'm a coward," he told the inky darkness surrounding the car. "Because I was afraid she'd say she is happy with her new life just the way it is and that she doesn't need another man showing up and complicating it."

He smacked the steering wheel with his fist and stepped down on the gas pedal and headed for home. It was the beginning of what promised to be another in a long string of sleepless nights.

Chapter 20

THE NEXT DAY, when a knock sounded on the front door, Faith had just finished feeding Lizzie supper and was sitting on the living room floor with her building a Lego tower. Despite her throbbing heart and swirling emotions, Faith pushed away a nagging surge of hope that it was Cole and opened the door.

Her father grinned at her. "Hi, Princess."

"Hey, Daddy. What brings you here?" She kissed his cheek, then stood back and let him enter.

He side-stepped Pup, who had come charging in at the sound of voices, then walked into the living room. When he spotted his granddaughter, he squatted down next to Lizzie who was busy taking apart the tower that Faith had just built.

"Hi, there. How's my favorite granddaughter?" Lizzie giggled and offered him a bright red block. "Well, thank you. I think we need to put that right here." He placed it carefully atop what was left of the tower then straightened. "Faith, I want to talk to you."

Faith's heart sank. She was always "Princess." He never called her by her given name unless it was something serious. "Okay. Let's sit in here so I can keep an eye on Lizzie." She motioned toward the couch. When they were both seated, she asked, "What is it?"

"We need to talk about your mother."

Faith couldn't imagine why her father had come to talk about her mother. Was she ill? Was he leaving her? Celia wasn't her favorite person, but she hoped none of her guesses for his visit were true.

"Daddy, what's going on?"

Her father looked down at his hands, then back to her. "Honey, there's something we never told you. But I think you need to know now. It might help explain why your mother is the way she is . . . the way she's been all your life."

Faith's stomach did a nosedive. She couldn't imagine what her father was going to tell her. Whatever it was, he was obviously having a hard time getting it out. "What is it, Daddy?"

His eyes welled up with moisture. "Before we had you, your momma and I had a baby boy. Teddy was his name."

Disbelief flooded Faith. Brother? She'd had a brother and no one had told her about him? She wasn't sure what she should be feeling. Anger that she hadn't been told? Regret that she'd never known him? Sympathy for her parents? She couldn't imagine what it would be like to lose Lizzie.

Emotions she couldn't define or control went wild inside her. Still unable to believe what she was hearing, Faith shook her head. "I don't understand, Daddy. I . . . have a brother?"

"*Had*, sweetheart." Her father's voice cracked. He cleared his throat. "He died when he was just a few months old. Something to do with his heart." She opened her mouth to speak, but her father stopped her with a raised hand. "I know this is a shock, but let me finish."

Her heart went out to this man who obviously still mourned the loss of his son. She sat back, ready to listen. Eager to hear about this brother she never knew.

"Your mother didn't take it well. She went into a deep depression and buried herself in the church." He ran his hand through his hair. "I took her to a doctor, and he gave her medicine, but she never liked taking it. Said it made her foggy. When she had you, I hoped that things would change, but they didn't. Under the guise of her newfound religion, she protected you by limiting your activities and keeping you as close to home as she could."

He stood and walked to stand beside Lizzie. He looked at the child with so much love in his expression that it took Faith's breath away. "After I was here the other day, I went home and told her about our granddaughter and how beautiful and sweet she is. When she said she'd have nothing to do with the 'devil's child', I gave her a choice. Either she takes her meds or I leave."

Faith was stunned. She didn't know what to say. So many things were running through her mind, she couldn't make sense of any of it. She looked around the room as though the answers she sought were hidden somewhere in the shadowy corners. But they weren't.

When she finally found her voice, the words that came out weren't the ones her heart wanted her to say. They were the caustic words of a woman who had been betrayed again. "How could you do this? How could you not tell me? How—"

Her father rushed back to the couch, sat, and took her hands in his. "Princess, you have to understand. It wouldn't have solved anything to tell you. It wouldn't have brought your brother back or cured your mother." Tears ran down his cheeks. "Try to find forgiveness in your heart. Sometimes, even though we don't intend to, even though it's the farthest thing from our minds, our actions inadvertently hurt the very people we love and want to protect most.

"Your mother was sick when she hurt us, but she's been back on her medicine for a few days now, and she's better." He smiled weakly. "She's slowly becoming the girl I fell in love with and married.

"I love you, Princess, and I'm so very sorry I never made your life easier. I never wanted you to know that your mother was sick." He kissed her forehead and stood. "I know I've given you a lot to think about, but now that she's on her medication, I think your mother will come around. I think she can be the grandma this sweet baby should have. All I ask is that you give her a chance to prove it."

Faith never saw him leave. She only vaguely recalled hearing the door close behind him.

LIKE A ROBOT, Faith got Lizzie into bed, cleared up their supper dishes, walked Pup, and straightened her house. Hoping busy work would keep her from thinking, she decided to give Pup a bath. But even the squirming, soapy puppy couldn't keep her from thinking about all her father had told her. By the time she'd finished bathing and towel-drying Pup, showered, put on her nightgown, and then climbed into bed, she still couldn't wrap her mind around what she'd heard.

A brother.

She'd had a brother, and her parents hadn't told her. Even as she strained to remember if there had been anything, any object in the house that would have told her about Teddy, she could think of none. Perhaps erasing all traces of the baby was her father's way of helping her mother heal.

But it certainly explained why her mother had been like she was while Faith was growing up. If she lost Lizzie, she wasn't sure how she would continue to live, much less go on with her life as if nothing had happened. She now understood why her mother had kept her only child on such a short leash and monitored her every move. She'd probably been terrified of losing another child.

What surprised her was that her father had stuck by her mother for all those years. It couldn't have been easy. But he had. He'd loved and protected her through it all, much as Cole had protected her and Lizzie through everything that had happened to her since she'd gotten back to town.

Thoughts of Cole brought back the longing she'd felt when he'd left after she'd found the money. He'd always been there for her and maybe, if he was here, he could help her sort through all this. But she'd driven him away with her foolish inability to trust.

Suddenly, Faith sat up straight in bed. It was never Cole she hadn't trusted. It was herself she hadn't trusted and the belief that all the men in her life had betrayed her in some way. First her father, who had never stood up for her with her mother. But, right or wrong, he'd felt he'd been protecting his daughter from knowing about the sickness her mother was struggling with. Then Sloan. But she'd known almost from the beginning that Sloan was less than honest, and she'd stayed with him anyway because she loved her daughter and didn't want her to grow up fatherless.

Sometimes, even though we don't intend to, even though it's the farthest thing from our minds, our actions inadvertently hurt the very people we love and want to protect most.

Her father's word rang through her head like a tolling church bell. Had Cole intended to tell her about the letter? Instead of running away like a petulant child, why hadn't she given him a chance? Without overwhelming her, he'd done nothing but protect and take care of her and Lizzie since the day he'd stepped foot in Doc Amos's office. He'd saved her daughter's life when she'd almost gotten bitten by a poisonous snake. He'd given Faith independence by teaching her to drive and making sure she had a car and providing her with a cell phone. Why was she allowing a stupid letter to come between them?

She picked up her cell phone off the night table and started to punch in Cole's number, but paused and glanced at the clock. Reluctantly, she replaced the phone on the table and then switched off the lamp. Since it was the middle of the night, her breakfast of crow would be better served in the morning.

COLE SAT ON HIS porch, a cup of coffee getting cold in his hands. Little to no sleep the night before had left him feeling less than human. But he couldn't get Faith off his mind. All he could think of was how frightened she'd been, and that he hadn't been there to protect her. How she'd trembled in his arms and sobbed until his shirtfront was soaked with her tears.

He stared at the lavender clouds drifting across the horizon, their undersides pink with the dawn. Very slowly, the sun rose above the mountains, painting everything with glorious light. Morning birds began to chirp and gather at the feeder.

Normally, he loved to watch the dawn break, but today, his thoughts were far down the mountain in a little house with a woman and a precious little girl. How he'd grown to love them both. Then, because of a stupid letter and his neglect in not telling Faith about his plan to go and his decision not to move away, he'd lost it all.

He should have forced her to listen to his explanation. Instead, he'd let her walk away and when he'd had the opportunity again to talk to her about it, he'd walked away.

So, what's holding you back from telling her now?

"Nothing!" He stood, set his cold coffee on the porch floor, then reached in his pocket for his car keys.

The sound of a car coming up the mountain stopped him. He concentrated his gaze on the spot in the driveway where a car would appear if it were coming to his house. Moments later, the car edged into his yard. When he saw who it was, his breath caught in his throat, and his heart began to pound as if it would fly out of his chest. His grip on his keys tightened.

Faith!

FAITH PARKED THE car and just sat there staring at Cole, drinking in the sight of him like a woman dying of thirst. The sun illuminated the expanse of his muscular chest and arms and picked up the blue highlights in his coal black hair. The man was enough to take any woman's breath away.

Having put off what she'd come here for as long as she could, she climbed from the car and made her way across the lawn, then up onto the porch. She stopped beside him. "Good morning."

"Good morning. What brings you here so early?"

For a moment, she studied him, trying to gauge his mood. But his face was as blank as an unused sheet of paper. But she bit the bullet. "We need to talk."

He turned and sat down in one of the white rockers, then motioned for her to join him in the other. "What do we need to talk about?"

Well, at least he wasn't turning her away. Not that he shouldn't after the way she'd treated him. "The letter." She glanced sideways at him, then out across the lawn to the far mountain. "We need to talk about the letter."

When Cole said nothing, she felt a cold spasm clutch her heart. He'd given her a chance to hear him out, and she'd denied him that opportunity. Maybe she wouldn't get a second chance.

"What about it?"

She cleared her throat, but continued to look out over the landscape, afraid of what she'd see in his eyes. "You wanted to explain about it, and I wouldn't let you." She turned toward him, but still avoided his eyes. "I'm really sorry I behaved so childish and unfair, but I'm ready to listen now if you still want to tell me."

"Are you sure you want to hear it?"

Faith wasn't sure she *wanted* to, but she needed to hear it. Even if it ended with her going home alone. She smiled. "I dropped Lizzie off at Granny Jo's so we'd have time to talk. Yes, I want to hear it. The whole story."

Cole stood and went to sit on the railing facing her. "I worked for the Richmond PD before I moved back here. At first it was a great job, exciting, adventuresome. All the things the TV shows depict." He gazed off the side of the porch, as if peering into a past only he could see. "Then I saw things. Things I'll never forget. Charred bodies that were pulled from buildings that were nothing but ashes. Old women killed for their Social Security checks." He shook his head as though to dislodge the pictures in his mind. "The final straw was when I was called to the multiple homicide of a mother and her two young children. I knew then that I couldn't keep going if I wanted to retain my sanity."

The pain in his voice and the darkness in his eyes tore at Faith's heart. She had to force herself to stay in the chair and not run to him, hold him, and give him some of the solace he'd given her so many times. Instead, she remained where she was.

He took a deep breath. "So I decided to leave law enforcement and use my degree in history to teach. But then my father got ill and asked me to step in for him. So I did, but I had already put in my application to teach at an Atlanta high school. The plan was to come here and fill in for him until the election, then move on to the teaching position. The letter you saw was to tell me about an orientation day for new faculty, but I called them and refused the job. I'm staying in Carson and running for sheriff."

Relief flooded through Faith like a spring thaw. But she

warned herself about jumping to conclusions. Faith screwed up her courage to ask the question she hoped would tell her how Cole felt about her. "So what happened? Why did you decide to stay?"

He left the seat on the railing and squatted down in front of her. "One of the things I wanted most in life was a family of my own. I never thought I'd get that. Then I met a beautiful woman and a precious little girl who stole my heart."

She could feel his breath on her face. "Just the little girl?" Her voice came out barely a whisper.

"No. I fell in love with her mother, too."

Before she could say anything, he leaned toward her, and then whispered, "And I think she might love me, too."

Faith released a breath she hadn't even been sure she was holding. "Oh, she does. She absolutely does."

He gathered her in his arms, lifted her from the rocker, and then kissed her like he'd never stop.

Epilogue

Three months later

SO FAR, FAITH'S wedding day had turned out perfectly. The cloudless blue sky hung over Hawks Mountain like a good omen. An autumn breeze still carrying the breath of summer blew through the open church windows. It had stayed warm enough to open the building's doors and windows, allowing the mountain air inside to spread the sweet perfume of the flowers that lined the altar. And best of all, she was about to marry the man of her dreams, a man she loved and who loved her in return.

She spun in front of the full-length mirror that had been placed in Reverend Thomas's study just for the wedding. The silk and lace skirt of her wedding gown flared out around her and made it appear as though she floated inside a fluffy white cloud.

"Stop fussing. You look beautiful." Becky Hart, Faith's maid of honor, stood behind her. "I'm sure Cole will be absolutely blown away." She checked the wall clock and then handed Faith her bouquet of white roses, baby's breath, and stephanotis. "It's almost time to go."

Faith gripped the handle of the flower piece, her heart beating triple time. In a few minutes, she'd be Mrs. Cole Ainsley. She still had an overwhelming urge to pinch herself to make sure she wasn't dreaming.

The study door opened, and her father stepped into the room, looking dapper in a black tuxedo. "Ready, sweetheart?"

"Ready, Daddy." Faith took his arm.

"You look beautiful." He beamed at her, kissed her cheek, patted her hand, and then led her into the vestibule.

The organ music began and, as they entered the aisle laid with a white silk runner, Faith spotted Cole standing at the altar. Her breath caught in her throat. How had she won this handsome man for her own? Keeping her gaze centered on Cole, she clung to her father's arm and followed Becky up the aisle. Everyone else in the small church faded away. There was only Cole, his face alight with love.

Most of the ceremony was a blur. Faith heard her voice repeating the vows, then Cole's deep voice repeating his, and him sliding a ring on her finger. His kiss was whisper-soft and filled with promises of all their tomorrows.

From somewhere beyond the small circle of happiness surrounding her and Cole, Faith heard her daughter say, "Papa."

A mother's instinct made Faith turn to see what her daughter was up to. A wave of shock coursed over her. Hardly able to believe her eyes, she clutched Cole's hand for support.

Sitting beside her father in the front row was Faith's mother, holding Lizzie on her lap. For a moment, Faith could only stare. Then her mother smiled. Faith handed Cole her bouquet and reached behind her neck to unclasp her necklace. Silently, she walked to her mother, leaned forward, and then clasped the necklace around her mother's neck.

"Thank you . . . Mom."

With tears glistening in her eyes, Celia smiled hesitantly and touched the gold pendant. "Thank you." It was just a whisper, but for Faith, it was as loud as if her mother had shouted it from the top of Hawks Mountain.

Faith's heart swelled. For a girl who hadn't believed in them, it looked as though she had finally found her bright tomorrows.

The End

Granny Jo's Journal

I can't believe the summer's sped by so fast. But at least it ended on a very happy note—Cole Ainsley's and Faith Chambers' wedding. I love weddings, especially when it means a happy ending for two people so deserving of it, and Faith and Cole are just such people. It was a beautiful affair, and I'm tuckered out from dancing, and full to busting from eating the delicious dinner they had at the reception and following it up with a big slice of wedding cake.

It just pleased me no end to see Celia Chambers there. I'm not sure she'll ever shed her holier-than-thou attitude, but at least she's washed a bit of the starch out of her britches. And Horace looked proud as punch to be giving his lovely daughter away. I have a feeling, with both of them showing Lizzie so much love, that I won't be babysitting for that little one much anymore. And that makes me a little sad, but also pleased as a spring foal in a field of new grass. The little ones need their grandmas and grandpas.

The only thing about the whole day that bothered me was when I spotted Jacy Brooks sitting all by herself. She hasn't been the same since her husband Steve died. Lord knows, I understand better than most how it feels to lose the man you love, and how you just want to give up on life and hide. But as my Earl would say, you can't live in the grave. I was surprised she was even at the wedding. Most times, she just stays locked away in that old farm house they were renovating. Breaks my heart. I'll say a prayer for her that she finds her way back to happiness.

On a happier note, Faith tells me that she's gonna use the money her grandmother hid inside that teddy bear to open a nursery school. Lord knows Carson could use one. There are a lot of new parents in town who have to work to make ends meet, and a nursery school run by a loving mother would be just the thing. I'll never understand why Connie Harrison put the money inside the bear, but it was nothing short of a miracle that that wolf puppy tore that bear apart so they found it. Faith has asked me to work with her at her nursery school, and I'm tickled pink at the prospect of spending the day surrounded by little ones.

Well, I'm worn out from all the excitement today, so I best be off to bed. But I'll be right here the next time you find yourself visiting my little town.

Blessings,

—*Granny Jo*

About Elizabeth Sinclair

Elizabeth Sinclair is the award-winning, bestselling author of numerous romance novels and two acclaimed instructional books for writers. Her novels have been translated into seven languages and are sold in seventeen countries. She lives in St. Augustine, Florida, with her husband and two dogs. Elizabeth is the mother of three children and "brags constantly" about her grandchildren.

Visit her at ElizabethSinclair.com

CPSIA information can be obtained
at www.ICGtesting.com
Printed in the USA
FFOW02n0125090914
7239FF